# GOON

# GOON

## Edward Lee
## &
## John Pelan

Overlook Connection Press
2003

GOON
©1996 by Edward Lee and John Pelan

Dust Jacket Illustration © 2003 Erik Wilson
Interior Illustrations © 2002 Micha Hayes

Published by
Overlook Connection Press
PO Box 1934, Hiram, GA 30141
www.overlookconnection.com
overlookcn@aol.com

Hard Cover
ISBN: 1-892950-63-4

Signed Sterling Edition of 100 copies and 26 Full Grain Leather
Lettered Editions Published simultaneously

First Edition

Book Design & Typesetting:
David G. Barnett/Fat Cat Design

ACKNOWLEDGMENTS:
Jonathan Snowden, Tony Gancarski, Lee Casebolt, Matt Cleary, CRZ, Survival Parkhurst, Dan the Masked Graduate, STUART, Dr. K, Dean~!, Mike Naimark, The Two Phils, Pogo Pete Stein, Rev Ray, Canz, JDW, BostonIdol, and all the regulars at tOA and DVD.

J.P


To Dave Barnett, for the great job on the first edition; to Dave Hinch for this great job on the second.

E.L.

# INTRODUCTION
## T. WINTER-DAMON

irst, let me openly admit that, in delving into the darkest regions of the human consciousness, in exploring the most demented extremes of perversity and aberrant behavior—a task I've committed myself wholeheartedly to in creating my own somewhat notorious body of works—an undesirable side effect is I've become quite jaded when it comes to horror fiction (and film, too, for that matter). Regardless of their pandering promises of gut-wrenching terrors, there is very little I read or see that draws more than a bored *ho hum* of ennui...

So very little to match those sick, feverish sensations of dread gleefully suffered while surviving a first encounter with, say, the writings of the Marquis de Sade, or Jack Ketchum's **Off Season**, or Wes Craven's **The Last House on the Left**, or Tobe Hooper's original **The Texas Chainsaw Massacre**, or George Romero's **Night of the Living Dead**, or David Cronenberg's **They Came from Within,** or Pier Paolo Pasolini's **Salo**, or Jorg Buttgereit's **Nekromantik**, or John McNaughton's **Henry: Portrait of a Serial Killer**, or the ripoff **Confessions of a Serial Killer,** or such classics of seemingly "unredeeming social value" as those beloved Herschell Gordon Lewis' sick-flicks like **Blood Feast, 2000 Maniacs, A Taste of Blood, The Wizard of Gore**, and **The Gore Gore Girls**...? or their diseased offspring such as **Blood Diner, Bloodsucking Freaks, Doctor Butcher, M.D., Don't Go in the House, I Spit on Your Grave, Last House on Dead End Street, Maniac, Mark of the Devil**, and **Street Trash**...

In part, I suppose, the fault lies in that we live in an age of utter hypocrisy—an age of false Puritanism and sham prudery, of the Moral

Minority, where, although our newspapers and newscasts scream with closeups of bloody atrocity after bloodier atrocity, and the statisticians regale us daily with the ever-climbing percentages of teen violent crime and teen and preteen sexual activity and resultant pregnancies and AIDS infected casualties, try "pushing the envelope" in film or fiction, in these areas, and you'll find out just how conservative/uptight The Establishment can be...Look at how Hollywood censorship chewed up the celluloid release of the "too sadistic overtones" present in the original, script-based cut of Dave Schow's **Texas Chainsaw Massacre III**!

**THIS "MORALISTIC" BIG-BROTHERING IS TOTAL BRAINDEAD BULLSHIT! YOU DON'T LIKE THE BOOK, YOU DON'T LIKE THE MOVIE—DON'T READ IT! DON'T WATCH IT! RIGHT...?**

*Okay. Okay. I'm down off my fucking soapbox, all right, already...?*

*Heh.* In case it hasn't hit you yet, think about *this—*

only *2* of the gutwrenchers I listed were *books*, the rest were all splatterfilms...*right?*

So. Who *does* deliver a total, no-holds-barred, bloody, puking bodyslam of a read in the world of horror fiction...? These guys and ladies can't all be pussies and limpdicks, can they...?

Chances are, if you're holding this book in your hot, sweaty palm, right now, then we might ASSUME you already know, *right...?* But, then again, you know the standard caveat regarding "ASS-U-ME", don't you. I mean, you *might* just be a pro-wrestling fan who picked this up thinking, "O, goody! a nice little book about Hulk Hogan and Sting and Hacksaw Jim Dugan and Macho Man Randy Savage and the Undertaker and The American Dream and all their ring-buddies... *right?* I mean, *anything's possible...*

No. I don't mean Charlie Grant. I don't mean Ray Bradbury. Nor Ray Russell. Nor William F. Nolan. And I sure don't mean Dean Koontz...

I *could* be referring, perhaps, to those high-visibility Splatter Dudes, like Clive Barker, John Mason Skipp and Craig Spector, David Schow, Ray Garton, R.C. Matheson, Joe Lansdale, the Michael Slade consortium, or (mutual pal) Killer Rex Miller...

But, quite honestly, none of these guys comes anywhere *close* to the writer in question, when it comes to being the true literary inheritor of the Herschell Gordon Lewis' filmschool legacy...the **UNDISPUTED, HANDS-DOWN KING of the MONDO GROSSOUT**...

I believe most readers familiar with the more extreme fringes of modern horror would agree. There is only *one* writer whose works I always approach with that same frisson of anticipatory terror, that same sick, thrilling knotting of the stomach I felt as a child.

Okay.

Enough tapdancing.

**EDWARD LEE KICKS BUTT!**

Nobody.

I mean NOBODY, writes as consistently heatedly-explicit, over-theedge, bloodbathing, gutwrenching, hardcore horror as EDWARD LEE. He pulls no punches. Takes no prisoners. Makes no apologies. **He WANTS to GROSS YOU OUT! BUGFUCK YOUR BRAIN! MAKE YOU PUKE! BIGTIME!** And *he never, never fails to deliver...*

Consider his published kickass novels—**GHOULS, INCUBI, SUCCUBI, COVEN, CREEKERS, THE CHOSEN**, and (under the pseudonym "Richard Kinion") **SACRIFICE**. Consider Lee's release from Necro Publications—**HEADER**. Consider his short stories, like his notorious Stoker finalist, "Mr. Torso", from **HOT BLOOD IV, DEADLY AFTER DARK**...

If that's what you're looking for in horror, then **GOON** will prove no disappointment. I guarantee you. Next to his novel, **THE BIG-HEAD**, I believe **GOON** is the most nauseatingly repulsive, dementedly perverse can't-put-it-down-no-matter-how-much-you-want-to page-turner to yet bear his name, chock full of sex-u-ral deviates and muckjumpin' bughouse schizoid freaks, and psycho possum-chompers from Hell...

Now, Edward Lee is one sick, corpsegrinding fuck of a writer, but you tagteam him with another stone twisto, chainsaw-huggin' whackadoo like the notorious Darkside Press' Editor/Publisher John Pelan—the same psycho who brought you the **DARKSIDE: HORROR FOR THE NEXT MILLENNIUM** anthology and such demented collections as Wayne Allen Sallee's **WITH WOUNDS STILL WET**—and add to that not only Pelan's creative proclivities for the perverse but also his preeminent knowledge of the wrestling scene (this guy is actually *friends* with some pro wrestlers!)—you're in for one gut-grabbing rollercoaster ride to Hell, *count on it...*

I kid you not, reading **GOON**, I could barely tolerate the mere *sight* of food for nearly two days afterwards...

I confess. It was the sex scene between Officer Straker and Ghoula that did it for me...

I mean, this shit could *damn near* turn a stone horndog pussyhound *celibate* for *life...*

So, hang on, have some truly devilish, demented fun, and get ready for one HELLUVA GROSSOUT...

And, to paraphrase the immortal/immoral words of the Granddaddy of Gore, *hisself,* Herschell Gordon Lewis, just keep tellin' yourself:

"It's only a book! It's only a book!"

FINAL CAVEAT: It may be. But I'd still keep a pack of those industrial-strength airline flightbags handy!

TRUST ME...

t. Winter-Damon,
Prophet of the Perverse,
Tucson, Arizona
10 July 1996

# PROLOGUE

"I liked that."

Felander shuddered as he watched the tall man put the last of seven stitches into his torn lip. The man hadn't even removed his mask for the operation. The dead, flat nailhead eyes peered from the typical red canvas shell, with glittery blue trimming. Just his ruined mouth and flat, dead eyes exposed.

"Who do I wrestle tomorrow?"

"Slick Dare, Luntville," Felander answered. But this was obligatory too. He wasn't thinking about tomorrow night's card. "An easy work. You come after him with a bat, then he snatches it and hits you in the head. Same gimmick as the last three cards."

"Um. Fine." The mammoth figure turned, disappearing behind the scarlet curtain. "Good night."

*Yeah, goodnight.* Felander winced when he looked at the mutilated body on the floor. *What a mess,* he thought.

⊛ — ⊛ — ⊛

The black Winnebago rumbled down the road. Trees on either side splintered the moonlight, a lambent webwork glissading over the vehicle's black-lacquered finish.

*Just a nice quiet ride through the woods,* Jon Felander thought behind the wheel. Things could be worse, couldn't they? He couldn't wrestle anymore himself—blown knee. The promotion was about to get rid of him as manager for the big names like Dare and Ghoula and Funk. *You've lost your spark, Jon,* Virgil Watts had told him. But then Felander had brought in the spark.

And, besides, the money wasn't bad. It was just these late-night drives that bothered him, and of course the clean-up duties.

The Winnebago slowed at a spur on the road. Crickets chirruped when he rolled down the high window and tossed the bag into an adjacent ravine.

There was a tiny splash in the night, then the massive vehicle pulled off.

The bag contained two human hands and feet, twenty-eight teeth, and two eyeballs.

# PART ONE

L ee couldn't believe he'd let Lucille talk him into coming to this. *A wrestling match, for Christ's sake.* Everyone knew this shit was fake, so what was the point?

"Isn't this great?" Lucille enthused.

"Yeah. Terrific."

But fake or not, Luntville Coliseum was packed. For a whopping seven bucks a pop, they had the best seats in the house, front row, center ring—so close you could smell these guys. When one took a face slap, their sweat flew out and sprayed you. Right now, amid a cacophony akin to the Superbowl, two guys were hamming it up fierce in the so called "Squared Circle," some big guy with bleached blond hair and a bigger guy in a mask. The fans went wild, everything from ten year-old kids to senior citizens. Lee watched unimpressed as the guy in the mask picked up the blond and slammed him to the canvas with what the announcer called a tombstone pile-driver. The larger man then picked the prone grappler up in what Lee recognized as an airplane spin and tossed him deftly out of the ring.

"So who's Blondie?" Lee asked. "He's the good guy, huh?"

Lucille rolled her eyes at his ineptitude. "That's Slick Dare, and he's the Face."

"The Face?"

"That's what they call good guys. Faces. Bad guys are called Heels."

*You learn something new every day,* Lee reasoned, and dug into his box of popcorn. Intermittent glances, though, nagged at him. The guy in the mask—The Heel, Lee corrected himself—had just jumped off the top rope and somersaulted toward this blond guy named Dare. At the last moment, Dare jerked away and the masked guy landed belly-first on the concrete floor. The fans exploded.

"Did you see that?" Lucille remarked. "Still think this is all fake?"

"Come on," Lee replied. "The Heel dove out of the ring and landed on the floor. Big deal. These guys train for years to take falls."

Then—

*thwack! thwack! thwack!*

Lee watched as the Heel repeatedly smashed a metal folding chair against the top of Dare's pristinely blond head. "They're special chairs," Lee insisted. "They look real but they're actually made of plastic. I can't believe how fake this shit is."

Lucille scowled at his pessimism but then shrieked in glee as Slick Dare suplexed the masked guy on the cement floor. He turned and bowed to the cheering crowd. Behind him, the Heel rose, hauling a baseball bat out from under the ring. Lucille screamed and pointed: "Slick! Slick! Behind you!"

Naturally, Mr. Dare didn't hear Lucille, nor did he seem to hear the several thousand other people screaming the same warning. At the last moment, he turned, snatched the bat away from the Heel, and—

*Ka-KRACK!*

—broke it over the Heel's head.

The applause deafened Lee as Slick Dare jogged back to the dressing room, arms raised in victory in spite of the disqualification. Two men in white came out with a stretcher, and began lifting the Heel onto it.

"How's that for fake?" Lucille challenged.

Lee laughed. "You kidding me? He hit the guy in the head with a balsa wood bat. You couldn't hurt a lady bug with that thing." But just as he'd finished the statement, something touched his foot. Lee looked down.

It was the fat half of the broken bat.

*I'll prove it's balsa wood,* he thought, and picked it up.

And pick it up he did, his eyes widening at the feel of its weight and density. Ash splinters jutted sharply from the break, and Lee knew at once.

*This ain't balsa wood. Jesus Christ. This is a real fucking Louisville Slugger...*

His gaze trailed off, watching the two guys in white lug the Heel away on the stretcher.

Lee dropped the broken bat with a sick sensation in his gut. "What, uh, what's that guy's name?"

"I told you, Slick Dare." Lucille grinned. "Isn't he handsome?"

"No, no, not him, the other guy. The Heel."

"Goon," she said. "His name is Goon."

✲ — ✲ — ✲

The flood of semen eddied into Melinda's mouth. Her eyes squeezed shut. For a moment, she feared she might gag and blow all the sperm out her nose.

"Yeah, oh shit, honey," Reed said. The big black hands gripped her head like a vise. The penis in her mouth felt like a baby pig. Melinda thought it was going to push all the way down into her stomach when he came. *Gimme a break!* she thought.

"Aw, yeah." Eventually he pushed her mouth off. "Gonna be a good girl and swallow, right?"

Melinda gulped it down, wincing. She should be used to it now; it all tasted pretty much the same: like thin, hot snot. She sighed and leaned back. Reed the Butcher sat down on the bed. He grinned slyly. "You ringrats sure can suck a cock, oh yeah. You oughts to have a belt, baby: Deep South Conference Cock-Suck Champ."

"Thanks," Melinda said. "You really know how to flatter a woman." After nearly a month of this, Melinda Pierce figured she could now call herself a full-fledged ringrat. She was willing to do whatever it took to get what she wanted, and there was one thing she wanted in a big way:

Goon.

The trail of broken, abused bodies was too obvious. She knew it was him; his handiwork was unmistakable. The only problem was...

Finding the big son of a bitch.

Unabashed at her nakedness, she lounged back on the motel bed, reached for her bottle of Canada Dry to wash the fetid taste of Reed the

Butcher's Man Batter out of her mouth. But when she glanced aside, she couldn't believe what she was seeing.

"What are you doing?" she exclaimed.

Reed, still in a sitting position, urinated gustily into the carpet. "Pissin', baby. What's it look like?"

"You ever heard of a toilet?"

Reed guffawed. "Shee-it, honey. This whole fucking $30-a-night motel is a toilet."

The stream of urine churned rents into the pile. It looked to be about a gallon. All Melinda could do was shake her head.

But she mustn't forget her purpose. *So what if the guy just pissed on the rug? I've got to find out about—*

"Hey, baby. Ya know, I got some good friends down the other end of the motel. Cool guys, all of 'em, and they won't try no shit, lemme tell ya. But-what'cha think? You interested in pullin' a train?"

A train. *Christ,* she thought. A choo-choo train. A gang-bang. Melinda had heard that ringrats do stuff like that all the time. She didn't quite understand the phenomenon. Sexual attraction was one thing, but… Shit. These guys were mostly dopes. Fucking brain-dead morons, but the interlude with Reed had hardly satisfied her, and it was still early. Sure, most of these guys were morons, but they *did* know how to party. And most them were built, a lot of them, like Dare and Dude and Romeo—and this dolt here, Reed the Butcher—they had great bodies, plus they were quite frequently over-compensated for in the genital department. *But there's more to the attraction than that, isn't there?* Melinda thought. *That's what's so great about these guys.* Rough sex and all the sensations that a veritable cornucopia of drugs and booze could provide and she wanted to taste it all.

"A train, huh?" she said. "Well, I might be interested, but—"

"But what, baby?" Reed, then, without reservation, rubbed the deflated serpent that was his penis.

"I want to know who's going to be there, you know?"

"Well, like I said, they all cool guys. No rough stuff. Horrific Harry Haylor, Cactus Zack, Rockin' Randy Viper."

"What about…Goon?" she dared to ask.

Goon?" Reed gaped. "Aw, shit, girl. Don't's ya tell me you gotta thing for him! That big weirdo—he never hang out with us other grapplers. No one never see him. Shit, most any town we gotta show, afterward we all's hit the local bar and shoot shit. But Goon? No way. That man never join us. N'fact, I don't's think I ever heard him say more'n two words. I worked a card with the guy last year. Smacked him on the head with a two-by-four, and you know what that crazy fucker whispered to me in the next clinch? He said 'Hit me harder.' And, I means, this was a real two-by-four. You gots to be careful how you hit a guy, else you could wind up crackin' his skull or even killin' him. But this nut says 'Hit me harder.' So's I did, and I'se hit him hard. That fucker falls down like the work says to do, and I win the match. But I sees him in the dressing room a half hour later like nothing happened. Shee-it, girl. That guy Goon, he ain't right. I mean, I hit this guy hard enough to knock *me* out."

For whatever reason, this information did not surprise her. "I want to do Goon," she said. "I need to see him."

"Well you can foe-get that, girl. I just got done tellin' ya. The man don't go out."

*He don't go out, huh?* Melinda thought. *Tell that to the six girls he's already raped and murdered.*

Reed the Butcher gave a tilted grin, cock-eyed. "A'corse, you'se come to this party wiff me—ya know, have some fun wiff dah fellas—and one'a dem might's be able ta introduce ya to Goon's manager. What say, baby?"

*Cock is cock,* she reasoned. Melinda shrugged. "So where's the party?"

✪ — ✪ — ✪

"Holy motherfucking shit," Straker muttered. He winced, appalled, at the thin, naked thing on the morgue slab. The stick-figure shone pallid white in the overhead fluorescents: slat-ribbed, a couple of tattoos, breasts so small they appeared nonexistent. And the nipples… Straker squinted. "What happened to her—"

"It's my consensus," Beck replied, "that the decedent's areolae were bitten off." Jan Beck ran VSP's Criminal Evidence Section. The witchlike woman was a stoic veteran of death. Dull, deadpan eyes assessed the corpse from behind large-framed glasses. Black hair frizzed out like an explosion, and she spoke as though she had sinus problems. "The m.o.'s identical to the other six. Death resulted from a transect fracture of the number three and four cervical vertebrae. Russell County Sheriff's Department found her in a ravine off State Route 154. They called VCU when they took one look at her. But at least we got an ID this time."

Straker looked up. "The first six were all Jane Doe's. This one had ID on her?"

"That's a fact." Beck closed the hatch of an autoclave, no doubt sterilizing her post instruments. "Like the others, the perp threw her clothes out too." Then Beck approached another table on which lay some bloodied garments; with forceps, she picked up a pair of shiny silver hot pants. "Until now, he's made every effort to reduce the likelihood of name ID. Cuts off the hands and feet, pulls the teeth, removes the eyes, and never-never—has he left a wallet or purse or anything that would contain any identification. But this time he slipped up. We found her driver's license in the back pocket of these."

Straker frowned at the hot pants, then cast a glance at the remaining garments. There wasn't much. Black fishnet stockings, a pink haltertop, darker pink high heels. The clothes were another parity. Sleazy, tacky, like a city streetwalker, just like the others. Only problem was there *were* no real cities in Russell County, nor in Pulaski, Edmunds, or Danner—the counties where the other bodies were found. All hick jurisdictions. "Even roadhouse whores and strippers don't dress like this."

"How would you know, Captain?"

Straker declined an answer. A real sense of humor. "Okay, you ID'd her, great. So what's her name?"

"Susan Bilks, 28 years old. Lives in south county."

*Lives?* Straker thought. *You mean lived.* He looked again to the body, and quailed.

Footless, handless, eyes extracted from their sockets. Nipples bitten off. Wisps of stringy blond hair lay stuck to the sides of her head.

Straker turned away, lit a cigarette in spite of the NO SMOKING!

FLAMMABLE CHEMICALS! sign. "Was she raped, uh, you know, like the others?"

"You bet," Beck affirmed. "Somebody did a cock job on her that would make Caligula puke. Joy juice in every hole, and lots of it. The B524 peptide scan estimates that she had about 60 cc's of sperm in her stomach. I aspirated another 60 or 70 from her rectal vault, and her vaginal barrel? Shit, Captain, it was Cum City. The girl's cervical cap was ruptured; the guy's cock was in her cervix when he came. He blew his wax all the way up into her ampullas and fallopian tubes. Must've been a hundred c.c.s of jizz hemorrhaged up there. Our man comes enough for 20 guys, Captain."

Straker was wincing. The way Beck talked never failed to make him sick. "So it probably was 20 guys, Jan. You know, a—"

"A gangbang?" Beck shook her head. "64s like this? You know the ride. They take forever to get the lab results back. Who cares about a dead Jane Doe out in the boondocks? But CellMark Labs in Maryland came back with the DNA test on the jizz from the first three girls. It's all the same, a five-probe match each time. All that cock-snot was dropped by one man."

Joy juice. Wax. Cock-snot. Straker, a man of protocol, simply could not think in such terms. *Gangbangs? Cum City?* No. No.

"And I presume that the...sexual traumas occurred..."

Jan Beck nodded. "Post extremis, Captain. This party started after her neck was broken. Just like the others."

"Well then. I'll leave the...cock-snot to you, Jan," he said, "and get back to my own areas of expertise." A final, accidental glance at the savaged girl caught him like a hook in the face. The vagina gaped, the majora hanging like lunchmeat. The sphincter too yawned at him, so loose now in its post-rigor: a distended socket of flesh, and a trickle of remnant semen glistening there. Straker left the autopsy suite, made it halfway across the State Reserved Lot, before he bent over and displaced the entire contents of his stomach onto the asphalt.

✸ — ✸ — ✸

"Okay, great," she said. "You're Goon's manager." A *snick-snick-snick* sound seemed to emanate from her, chewing fruity gum as she talked. "But I ain't interested in Goon's manager. I'm interested in Goon."

Jon Felander ordered her another drink. *What's her name again? Mary? Marie? Shit.* "Well that's good, because Goon is interested in you."

"Oh, come on!" Her fruity breath gusted with her excitement. "Really? You mean Goon's noticed me?"

*Tell them what they want to hear,* Felander thought. "Yeah. After his match tonight with Rocky Morton, Goon caught a glimpse of you in the crowd. 'That brunette with the pink pants,' he said. 'See if she wants to party 'cos she's one hot gal.'"

The girl—Mary, Marie, whatever—absolutely squealed with delight. The crowd at the back bar looked over, which made Felander suppress a smirk. The last thing he wanted was attention. After all, he was taking the girl to her death.

*Not that she'll ever be seen again,* he reminded himself. These places were all the same: closest bar to the arena, which were almost always dives. After the match, most of the grapplers on the card would flock here for a shitface, and the ringrats followed them like flies on a shitwagon. Felander glanced over his shoulder. Ted Rodz hamming it up with Johnny Adams, Dashing Dick Dude arm wrestling with Rex Ruger. And ringrats everywhere in between.

"Okay, so what's the scoop?" Mary sipped her drink—a big sip. Then her hand found its way to Felander's lap. "You take me to Goon in exchange for what? Head? I give good head. If you don't believe me, ask half the guys in DSWC."

"No, it's not like that," Felander assured her. God knew, he'd had his share of ringat blowjobs. *I'd sooner stick my dick in a garbage disposal...*

Mary, Marie, Whatever—smirked. "Okay, you wanna fuck me first, fine. You and Goon wanna do a threesome with me, fine."

No dice there, either. A lot of these 'rats were cute, sure, but to say that they were well-used would be the all-time understatement in the history of human sexuality. Felander could think of nothing less enticing than putting his pride and joy into an orifice that had been reverted to a communal sperm-dump/human herpes culture.

"I'm game for anything. Just so long as Goon's in the picture. I'll take you on plus fifty other guys as long a Goon's at the end of the line."

"Trust me, will ya? Goon's not into all that kinky group stuff. He's strictly one-on-one, and he's waiting for you right now. Let's go."

She fidgeted on her chair, a like a little kid who'd just been told by daddy that he's taking her to the mall to see Santa. Only Santa, in this case, didn't come down the chimney.

✪ — ✪ — ✪

Her name, in actuality, was not Mary nor Marie nor Whatever. It was Maureen. Strawberry blond, 5'7", a nice 34B. Secretary by day, ringrat by night. Some people liked broccoli as opposed to string-beans—well, Maureen liked wrestlers as opposed to any other kind of man.

And Goon as opposed to any other wrestler.

She never bothered to even try to figure it. She'd had her share of typical flings and even romances—one redneck, loser, and no-account after the next. Even the down and dirty ones, the handsome ones, and the ones carrying big cock—they left her bored, yawning, unfulfilled.

But grapplers?

*They float my boat,* she thought, leaving the bar. Nothing turned her on more than some slick-chested, big-pec'd, 290-pound slab of hunka-hunka pro wrestler squashing her hot bod flat against a motel mattress like soft cookie dough under a roller, and humping her straight into next Tuesday. All that sweat-veneered suntanned skin, those big collops of muscle flexing, and one hard cock after the next ready to work her pussy into a hot, spasmodic frenzy. Even the fat ones—the Blobsy Twins, Moonshine Shane, Faultline—they lit Maureen up like an ember pot that wouldn't go out. Nobody did it like the grapplers, and there was still one grappler she had to have...

"Wait a minute," she said, halfway across the parking lot. "We're going the wrong way. The motel's over there."

Felander rolled his eyes. "Goon doesn't stay in these fleabag motels—are you kidding? Let me tell you something, Mary—"

"Maureen."

"Right, Maureen. But let me tell you something. Between DSCW and his tours in Japan, Goon pulls in half a million a year. He doesn't stay in a *motel*. He's got a big, lux Winnebago. Wait'll you see it. Like a penthouse suite inside."

*A Winnebago?* Maureen shrugged. A mobile home was a mobile home, but— *What the hell do I care? As long as I get my hands on Goon, I don't care if he lives in a garbage truck.*

Her nipples felt sharp as golf cleats in the zebra-striped halter. Her four-inch heels ticked on the asphalt. *Goon,* she thought. *Goon...* Her dream was about to come true. She pictured him in her mind: 6'7" at least, biceps like melons, and pecs the size of a couple of slabs of porterhouse. Maybe it was the mask that put the icing on this sexual cake of hers, a final trimming of mystery. She wondered what his face looked like but then realized she didn't care. Her fantasy needn't have a face, just a body, *that* body, a frame of skin, bone, and muscle that weighed more than a refrigerator—all on top of her at once, squashing her into bliss.

"Almost there," said this guy Felander. And what was his story? Most of the heel managers were part of the show, but this guy? She'd maybe only caught two or three glimpses of him since Goon came to DSWC. At least he wasn't an asshole like a lot of them—that pussy with the tennis racket, or Al Lubano with the rubber bands in his face and a belly hanging down like a bag of pine-bark mulch—and as lumpy. She'd fucked him once and he couldn't even get his cock in her, his gut was hanging down so low.

Her high heels ticked on. As she followed Felander through the dark parking lot, she could feel her feminine parts already stirring. Her beige-and-glitter hot pants fit on her hips so tightly that the seam of the crotch separated her vulva into halves. Each step caused a sensation like a finger there. Soon she felt drenched, her clitoris inflamed. *If we don't get to this goddamn Winnebago soon,* she fretted, *I'll be coming in my pants!*

"Here we are."

The Winnebago sat at the furthest corner of the parking lot, in the dark. It's black paint-job would've made it completely invisible were it not for the single faint-yellow light in the tiny side window. "Why park all the way out here?" Maureen asked. "You're practically in the woods."

"Goon likes his privacy," Felander said. "Come on. You ready?"

*If you knew what was going on in my pants, you wouldn't have to ask.* "Wait!" She paused to fix her hair up, adjust her top. Suddenly frantic.

"Don't be nervous."

"I'm—" She blushed. She *was* nervous. The man of her most torrid dreams—Goon—was just a few feet away on the other side of that metal door.

Felander opened the door. "Watch your step." Then he led her inside. Wide inside. A small a/c unit rattled from the sidewall. All of the walls, however, and the ceiling too, seemed odd—tiles of some sort, with pegs sticking out, at least a hundred pegs per tile.

"Soundproofing," Felander said. "Things can get pretty noisy in here if you know what I mean."

But Maureen was staring ahead. Before her hung a plush scarlet curtain.

Felander's hand touched the curtain. "Mary—"

"It's Maureen."

"Er, right. Maureen. Anyway, it's my pleasure to introduce you to—"

His hand pulled back the curtain.

"—Goon."

*My...God...* All Maureen could do now was feast her eyes on what stood before her. She gazed with the same adoration of a priest gazing upon Jesus Himself.

The icon stood before her wearing nothing but the mask and a jock-strap stuffed with so much cock it looked like he'd stuck a bag of donuts in it. Cream-filled. His pecks flicked once. The massive expanse of chest shined in a sheen of sweat, and his arms were as big around as her legs. The barrel-like abdomen protruded, huge but not an ounce of fat.

Felander stepped back toward the door. "Goon, meet Marie."

"Maureen!" she corrected.

"Right. Maureen."

Cool-blue irises appraised her through the eyeholes in the mask. And that big roll of cock satcheled in the jockstrap began to visibly shift as he looked at her.

"Hi," Goon said.

But what an odd voice. Just a whisper, and something effeminate about it, like a passive gay guy. One thing was obvious, though...

*He ain't gay,* she thought. *If he's gay, how come his dick's about to bust out of that jock just looking at me?*

"Well, I guess I'll leave you two to your fun," Felander said. "Nice meeting you, Marianne."

Then she heard the door click shut behind her.

"You're...very...beautiful," came Goon's peculiar whisper.

Maureen nearly fainted. And she nearly came when that big, dinner-plate-sized hand reached out and gently touched her shoulder.

"Soft..."

So gentle... It shocked her. Goon stepped right up next to her. The big hands caressed her breasts through the zebra-striped halter, ran down her bare midriff, down her hips, and then back up again. Maureen closed her eyes and sighed. Wrestlers were usually rough—real rough. Maureen, like most ringrats, had been slapped, pinched, bitten, choked, spanked, gagged, blindfolded, tied up, gang-banged, play-raped, double-poked, fist-fucked, sodomized, etc. more times than she could remember. That's what she expected from wrestlers, and that's what she liked. She'd sucked asses and balls and toes. She'd had more cock in her mouth than Liberace and more jizz in her hair than shampoo. And in her time she'd probably engaged in the act of sexual intercourse more times than Marilyn Chambers. Gentle lovemaking wasn't her bag. She didn't want to hold hands in the park with these guys. She didn't want to be kissed and cuddled. She wanted to be balled till she bled, spewed in and spewed on, used as a thing for the primal pleasures of these looming, beefy behemoths.

In other words, she wanted to be treated like the fuck-pig she was, and that's why this was so strange she could hardly reckon it. Any other

guy and she'd be walking out the door right now, but this was Goon, and Goon was just so...

Different.

"Hold me," he whispered.

She put her arms around him—at least as best she could, for his girth prevented her hands from meeting. Just touching him like this made her feel electrified. His fingers, large as they were, tenderly stroked her hair, brushed her cheek, smoothed over the nape of her neck. Just as tenderly, then, he cupped her face and gazed so passionately into her eyes.

And then, just as tenderly—

*snap!*

—he wrung her neck.

"Traci Wilcox?"

Two eyes squinted through the gap, just over the safety chain. "Yeah? Who're you?"

Straker flashed his badge and ID card. "Captain Philip Straker. State Police. I need to talk to you about Susan Bilks."

"Aw, Jesus," she muttered beneath her breath. The door shut, the chain clinked, then she let him in. Decent joint for a double-wide trailer—decent at least in that it didn't stink like a month's worth of dirty diapers, backed up drains, and a month's worth of unwashed dishes. Straker, in the old days, must've answered a hundred domestics in trailer parks—drunken rube men beating the shit out of their drunken rube wives. The only things trashier than the occupants were the trailers themselves.

"So what happened?" Traci Wilcox griped, showing him into a cramped living room. "She get the shit beat out of her by one of them wrestlers?"

As Straker made to sit, he froze halfway down. "The shit beat out of her by *who?*"

The woman sat down with a sigh of disgust. Straker figured if he looked up the word "beat" in the dictionary, they'd have a picture of Traci Wilcox. Haggard, crow's feet, dark circles under her eyes. Central

Ident said she was twenty-nine but she looked ten or even fifteen years beyond that. She'd been a line-processor at Gronson's Chicken for a decade. Since the goddamn governor had deregulated the state's poultry industry in return for inside trading tips and campaign contributions spirited out of a corrupt S&L, the largest chicken producer in the country had become a legal sweatshop. Wilcox crossed her legs in the tattered corn-blue robe, hands crabbed like an old lady's from wringing guts out of #1 Whole Fryers for the last ten years. Tacky flip-flops hung off feet whose arches had long fallen flat, and the varicose veins in her legs looked like mapwork. She didn't seem to care that the top half of a drooping breast showed in the sagging v of the robe.

"Wrestlers, you know, pro wrestlers," she said.

"You're losing me, Miss Wilcox."

"She's a ringrat."

"A—"

"A ringrat. A wrestling groupie. Three or four nights a week, I swear to God, she dresses up in those whory outfits and goes to these goddamn wrestling arenas."

This was too bizarre. *Wrestlers?* "You're telling me that she dated professional wrestlers?"

"If *fucking* a bunch of over-built grapheads whenever they're in town means dating, then, yeah. I guess you could say that."

The expletive slapped him in the face. He couldn't imagine what she was talking about, but one thing was certain—

*She doesn't know,* Straker thought. *Damn it!*

"Listen, Miss Wilcox, before we go on, I regret to have to inform you that Susan Bilks is dead."

The walked-on face gaped, the pale parched lips opened, then closed. Her expression fell back to its dull, weathered platitude; her reaction to the news of her roommate's death had lasted no more than a second.

"Figures. Half of 'em are all fucked up on drugs is what I hear. It was only a matter of time before she got in over her head. I'll bet she was murdered, right?"

Straker thumbed his eyes, confused. "Yes, Miss Wilcox, she was murdered via an extreme mode of violence. Her neck was broken. She was mutilated. Not to mention, she was raped repeatedly, and I might add…"

Straker stalled. *No, no, don't tell her the rest.* You don't just walk in and tell someone her roommate was raped post extemis—after the point of death. You don't tell her that her hands and feet were cut off, her teeth were pulled out, her eyes were extracted—

No, you didn't tell them that.

But this was still too convoluted to contemplate. Straker may well have tripped over a lead. "Help me out here, Miss Wilcox. You're saying that Susan Bilks was…sexually involved with…professional wrestlers?"

Wilcox sipped lemonade from a smudged tumbler. Straker could easily smell that it had been tuned up with whiskey. "That's right. They call them ringrats—wrestling groupies. It's ridiculous. Susan was a cute girl. She could have pretty much any guy she wanted, but if it didn't have bleached-blond hair and wrestling trunks, she couldn't care less."

"Wrestlers," Straker stated baldly. He was still having a hard time with it.

"I didn't really know her, we just split the place—this is a double-wide, you know, forty-eight by thirty. I live on this side, she lives on the other. She was crazy about these dopes. Hell, one night she brought one back here—Kevin the Druid, she said his name was. Kinda short but real beefy, could barely fit in the door. Dark-sandy hair and a goatee— devilish-looking, and even I gotta admit, he was a turn-on. They go back in Susan's room and get started—Christ, I thought they were gonna knock the trailer off its bricks. All night long they did it."

This oddity, now, was beginning to coalesce. Straker didn't know wrestling from a hole in the ground. A stunt—that was his understanding, fake fights in an arena, characterized by phony rivalries. Each piece came as a separate thought: *Wrestlers. A wrestling groupie. Whory clothes.*

The first six bodies had never been ID'd, but…garments were found in their proximities, garments which certainly could be described as "whory." Hot pants, fishnet stockings, tight halters and tube tops, stiletto heels.

*Susan Bilks was a wrestling groupie. The first six girls must've been wrestling groupies too.*

Was it that easy? He walked into the home of this roughened chicken handler, expecting nothing. Yet Straker realized in a jolt that he was potentially one question away from solving the case.

"Miss Wilcox. If you can answer this next question, it might very well lead to the apprehension of Susan's killer."

She leaned over for her drink, unfazed. As she reached, the front of her robe opened wide enough to plainly show both breasts, which depended like white scrotums. Straker felt sure she was doing this on purpose. Their nipples more resembled wads of chewed raw beef.

"So what's the question?" she asked.

"If Susan was a wrestling groupie, it's clear that she went to a wrestling match on the night that she died. Our forensic technicians have determined with a fair degree of accuracy that she was killed three nights ago." Straker sat up at the edge of the seat to ask the question. "Do you know where Susan went three nights ago? Like *exactly* where she went?"

The tired shoulders shrugged. "Farling Civic Center, right downtown. Believe me, that's where she went every Wednesday night. There's always a match there. Seems to me that all you gotta do is find out which wrestlers were there on that night and you'll probably be able to figure out which one of the creeps killed her."

*Tell me about it.* Luck, in Straker's business, rarely played out this quickly. He rose, a bit dizzy. "Farling Civic Center. Thank you, Miss Wilcox. You've been very helpful."

The woman's eyebrows hitched. "Maybe, uh, well—"

Straker paused at the door. "What's that, Miss Wilcox?"

"Maybe there's something else I can help you with," she said, and with that remark she placed her flip-flopped feet up on the coffee table, and parted her legs. This, of course, afforded Straker a bull's-eye view of her genitalia.

His stomach shimmied. What he was looking at reminded him more of a pile of deviled ham stuffed into a cusp of hair.

"No thanks," Straker said. "I'm really in, uh, something of a hurry."

Next she fully parted the robe, showing the breasts which seemed to hang like men on gibbets. "In too much of a hurry to pick up Susan's diary?"

Straker's thoughts locked up. "Susan Bilks kept a diary? Miss Wilcox, that diary could be crucial to this case. I need that diary."

"And I'd be happy to give it to you, Captain…whatever your name is. But I need you to give me something in exchange."

*You gotta be shitting me!* She was blackmailing him. "That's coercion, Miss Wilcox, not to mention a grievous obstruction of jurisprudence. I'm a professional homicide investigator. You're asking me to commit an act of sexual turpitude that could jeopardize my job. Now you can give me that diary, or I can swear out a warrant and take it."

"Yeah, but who knows how long that would take?" Somewhere behind those tired, give-a-shit eyes something like hopeless longing raged. "All that paperwork and all? And who knows, in the time it takes you to get a warrant, that diary could become misplaced." She shrugged, sipped her drink. "It could even…disappear."

Jesus Christ! Straker winced, first at the sight of her putty-like breasts and the stacked-beef vagina, then at the thought of what he was about to do.

*What the hell,* he thought. *Couple of drinks first and it might not be so bad…*

❀ — ❀ — ❀

When Too Hot Romeo double-flipped off the top rope, Goon caught him in two beefy arms, then did the Back-Breaker. Too Hot, whose real name was Walter Rawson, feigned the appropriate level of pain, then rolled over, groaning. He felt ripped off, but what else could he do? *I'm the most acrobatic wrestler in the bizz, and now I'm doing mid-card matches for three-hundred a week.* He'd flunked three piss-tests in a row, so WCW had made an example of him. Doing all the anti-drug promo stuff in the ghettos didn't help; Too Hot often copped from the same dealers. So it was bye-bye to that 200 thou a year.

*It's because I'm black,* he felt convinced when Goon stomped his belly. Too Hot faked a near-rupture of the abdominal wall. *White oppression, racist motherfuckers.* Goon, then, pulled a full body splash off the ringpost, and Too Hot followed the script, rolling away just in time. The crowd cheered when he jumped up and landed a perfect drop-kick to this mastodon called Goon. He hit the canvas, covering Goon for the three count.

"You gotta hit me harder," Goon whispered, then jerked his shoulder up just before the last count. They hauled each other up in a clinch.

*Weird voice,* Too Hot thought, their heads locked. Kind of faggy. And how could he hit him any harder without knocking him out? "I did hit you hard," he whispered back.

Goon broke away then whipped brass knucks from his trunks. But Too Hot's expert side roll smacked Goon hard to the mat, and he twisted the knucks from the huge fingers.

"Real hard, right in the head," Goon whispered, faking his own shock. "You're grappling like a pussy."

Too Hot didn't like that. When Goon charged, he belted him a little too hard. Goon staggered but then charged again, locking up.

"What's the matter with you?" came the weird whisper. "These fans didn't pay to see paddycakes. Hit me hard with those knucks. Otherwise I'll turn this into a shoot and kick your ass for real."

"Think you can, asshole?"

Goon laid a chest slap that cracked through the arena like a gunshot. Too Hot lost his breath for a moment.

"What's your problem, shithead?" he hissed in the next clinch.

"You," Goon replied. "This is supposed to be a wrestling match, and all you're doing is prancing around like some home-boy shuck and jive nigger."

Too Hot's teeth clenched. "You better watch that shit."

"What? Nigger? Sorry, I meant to say porch monkey. Bet your mama's cookin' cornbread in some project, got about fifty welfare kids, huh?"

"You really want it bad, don't you, you big white piece of shit?"

"Yeah, I want it bad, so give it to me. I fucked your sister last night—what's her name? Lawanda, Sharonda, Linolium, some nigger name like that? She turns tricks at truck stops, ten bucks a pop. Lets nigger dealers knock her up so she can get more welfare. Or I should say *mo' weffair.* What's your favorite chicken, by the way? KFC or Popeye's? Lub dat dickin' at 'Op-eyes!"

By now Too Hot was burning up. Goon was goading him, the insidious whisper inaudible to the fans at ringside but each word stinging Too Hot like a slap across the face. Why was Goon doing this? *I could kill this guy with one solid punch in the head,* he realized. And if he heard the word *nigger* one more time, he just might do it.

"Got no balls, huh? Same as all you spooks," Goon continued to whisper. "I'm calling you a nigger to your face and you're not doing anything about it. Typical yellow-belly, no-balls cornbread-eating *nigger.* No wonder your people were slaves for three hundred years, no balls to do anything about it. Took a white man to get you out of the cotton fields. Ask me we oughta nuke all your goddamn nigger ghettos, get rid of all them crack babies and players selling coke to nine-year-olds, raping white women 'cos the nigger women are all three-hundred pound street cows slapping jive and buying sirloin with the welfare money whites give 'em. You'll be on welfare too, Sambo, after I break your knees so you can't wrestle anymore."

Too Hot seethed. "Call me nigger one more time and I'll crack your coconut with these brass knucks."

"Nigger. Why don't you go back to the 'hood, shoot some hoop, mug white people and panhandle in your $150 sneakers, and walk around like an asshole rubbing your crotch listening to gangsta cop-killer songs just like all the other useless, drop-out, thieving, crack-dealer niggers. Hey, blood, what up? Where dah white wimmins at? Where dah cornbread? Where 2-Pac?"

The red veil dropped. Prison would be next more than likely, or at the very least the final end to a career he'd already half-flushed down the toilet. Too Hot reeled back then—

*crack!*

—and landed a right hook into Goon's temple with the brass knuckles. The crowd roared. The bell clanged, and as the ref was disqualifying him, Too Hot Romeo belly-slid out of the ring and dashed for the locker room. *Gotta get out of here! I just killed that guy!*

He scrambled to dress in the locker room. Maybe he could head back to Denver, disappear and…well…sell drugs. It didn't really matter. Two refs brought Goon in on the stretcher before Too Hot could get out.

But then Goon sat up. "Hey, Too Hot. I was just joking with all that nigger stuff. Wanted to get you riled up, you know? The crowd loved that right hook."

Too Hot dropped his bag, stared in sheer disbelief that Goon was not only still alive but unhurt by a blow that would've certainly killed any man on earth.

⊛ — ⊛ — ⊛

Ketchum Athletic Center. Not much bigger than a high-school auditorium, and that's where half of DSWC cards took place—fucking high schools. *Talk about the pits,* Melinda thought. Fifteen ringrats congregated by the back door, fussing, cussing, whooping it up. Tonight's card was over—they'd be coming out soon, some to the nearest bar, others straight to the motel with a rat on their arm. In their heyday, most of DSWC's grapplers had lived the bigtime in WWF and WCW; Melinda had learned that much. Now they'd been consigned to this pissant federation because they were either too old or had stepped on too many toes in the bigger feds. *Goon could make a million a year in WWF,* Melinda realized, *but he's too smart for that.* A big contract would mean huge exposure, big cities, television. But by enlisting in the Deep South Wrestling Conference, it was just a bunch of boondock towns in boondock counties. Easy to hide. Less conspicuous. And the ringrats in these parts? Fly-by-nights. The kinds of girls nobody missed. Melinda knew Goon must be taking a girl at least once a week. And in these little redneck towns? So spread out? Not to mention the fact that only one of the seven victims thus far had even been identified, and there were probably seven more out there rotting in the woods, yet to be found. No doubt Goon's manager was taking care of body disposal, which meant that he was in on it too.

"I'm Pinkie," came a voice.

Melinda glanced aside. Blond, late 20s probably—ringrats generally weren't young. She chewed gum with enthusiasm, arms crossed beneath a ludicrous black-sequined top. Studded jeans, gaudy makeup. They all looked the same in a way.

"I'm Melinda."

"Who're you waiting for?"

"I don't know. Anything that looks good," she lied. Melinda need-ed to get close to some other rats, but she had to take it slow, gain their confidence first.

Pinkie snapped her gum, tapping her foot. "I'd like to snag Dick Dude, but I think he left after his match. I'm surprised they even put him on the card tonight. Dude's top-name now. Ketchum usually only gets the mid-names and jobbers."

"Hate to disappoint you, but Dude ain't worth shit in bed."

Pinkie gaped at her. "You—you've done Dashing Dick Dude?"

"Yeah," Melinda informed her. "Last month in Big Rock. Couldn't get it up to save his life. The steroids kill their dicks. Hunk Hargan's the same way. Dead dick."

Pinkie's tone turned skeptical. "Hunk Hargan's in WCW. They don't do matches down here."

"Back when I lived in Baltimore," Melinda maintained the lie. "My place was two blocks away from the Civic Center. Once a month WCW'd come to town, and so would WWF—big cards too, with all the names. We'd just wait for them outside the backstage door, and they'd pick us up in limos, takes us to this great bar by the airport hotel, the Safari Club it's called."

Pinkie's eyes widened in sheer envy. "Shit, I'd do anything to snag some real faces. Who... Who'd you get?"

Melinda shrugged as though it was no big deal. "Rex Ruger, The Big Bad Man, Shaun Jarrety, Undertow—a bunch. But I'll tell you, most of those big name guys in the big feds—they're all assholes. They're either cokeheads or steroid gobblers. At least the grapplers in the regional con-ferences are humble. I did Reed the Butcher the other night—pretty cool guy but, Christ, he was too big. I was walking funny the whole next day."

Pinkie giggled. "Better too big than not big enough. I got a crack at Rowdy Randy Rider right before he retired. He was great at first, put a pillow over my face, played like he was smothering me. But when I got a look—I swear!—it was only three inches! Hard!"

"Jeeze. I've seen bigger link sausages. Paul Smith's pretty small too, and so is Quake."

"Wow, you've done a lot of names. I never get to any of the big arenas 'cos I ain't got a car. Ketchum, Lockwood, Crick City—they're about the only places I can get to hitchhiking."

"My husband lost his job in Baltimore, worked for McCormick," Melinda practiced her undercover spiel. "So I dumped his ass and moved down here with my sister. It's a big difference going from WWF and WCW to this smaller fed stuff, but like I said—the big tv names? They're mostly schmucks. I keep hoping to snag Marcus Arelius or Too Hot Romeo. I did them both a couple of times back before they got kicked out of WCW for coke."

"What about Dare? You ever do him?"

"Naw, missed him every time, but he was losing his draw bad in WCW. I guess that's why he turned up in DSWC. Never lost the ego trip, didn't want to retire even though he's pigshit rich."

"Stylin' and profilin'!" Pinkie mimicked.

*Good,* Melinda thought. She was easing into conversation with credibility. Up ahead several rats squealed when the door opened, then a couple of jobbers walked out and took their pick. A moment later Harry Windingham strutted through the door, banned from the bigger feds for falsifying doctor's certificates. Melinda guessed it was better to be a big fish in a little pond than to be nothing at all. What could these guys do in the real world? *Probably not even smart enough to change tires.* Right after Windingham came The Invincible Cherokee— another has-been, so fucked up from steroids he sometimes couldn't remember his name. DSWC was the dust bin of the stars. Several more groupies paired off with them, and disappeared in low-rent hot rods.

"We're not going to get shit here," Pinkie regretted.

"Probably right. Too many rats and not enough grapplers."

Melinda figured the time was right. "Has Goon come out?"

"Goon? Eeew." Pinkie's face screwed up. "You like Goon?"

"Sure. Why not?"

"He gives me the creeps. One night in Lockwood I was blowing Fabulous Freddie Faylor in his Taurus and he told me Goon's the weirdest wrestler in the conference. Never talks to anyone, never goes out. He doesn't even stay in the motels, he and his manager live in a mobile home."

*A mobile home? Hmm.* There was some news, and that explained a lot. Harder to find, harder to nail down.

"Faylor said Goon must have some kind of padding or something under the mask, 'cos Freddie swears he hit him in the head with a chair hard enough to knock him out."

*You'd be surprised,* Melinda reserved the thought. "What else you know about Goon?"

"Zip. Oh, wait, I knew this one rat who said she talked to him once, and she said he must be queer 'cos he had a real femmy voice."

*Believe me, honey. Goon ain't queer.* "Know any way I might pick up on his manager?"

"Felander? Naw. Nobody ever sees him either, since he dropped the Shock and Roll Express. He managed Dare too for a little while, and the Fabulous Ghoula but dropped them the minute Goon came onto the scene. I can't see him making more money with Goon than names like Dare and Ghoula."

*That's because you don't know about Goon,* Melinda thought.

"Felander was friends with Kevin the Druid back around the same time," the girl continued. "I had Kevin once, but then he disappeared from the scene completely."

*He sure did.* Melinda looked behind her into the parking lot. "I guess Goon's gone 'cos I don't see any mobile home here."

"He always leaves right away's what I heard."

Shit. She'd been on this case a month now and was no closer to Goon since day one. *I've got to get to Felander. If I can get to Felander, I can get to Goon...*

Just then the back door chunked open and disgorged a fat security guard. "Let's clear it out, ladies," he addressed the few remaining rats. "Everyone's gone."

The congregation groaned in unison, then began to scuffle off in their high heels.

"Fuck," Pinkie said.

"Oh well," Melinda realized. "No sugar tonight. See ya later."

"'Bye."

Melinda walked off into the dark. *Waste of time,* she thought. *At this rate I'm never going to find Goon.*

# GOON

*—Goon. I've had exactly 107 grapplers, but he's the one I want the most,* the diary read in purple, cursive Flair Pen. *I've talked to tons of other rats, and nobody's had him, and I've gotten to a lot of grapplers just hoping one of them could fix me up with Goon, but—no dice. Most of the other grapplers are spooked by him, they say he's weird, they say he's scary. Ted Rotunda said he DDT'd Goon onto real cement once and blew the move, rammed Goon's head into the concrete for real, then said that Goon wasn't even fazed once he saw him back in the locker room. And Mike Debiase said the same thing. Goon's just a heel but he takes punishment like nobody else. Rumor is he's turned down big buck contracts with Japan, ECW, SMW, and even WWF, but he doesn't take them. He wants to stay a heel in DSWC, and that's it. But I guess that's his business. I don't care.*

*I don't care about anything except snagging Goon.*

Straker's eyes narrowed. He closed the diary, perplexed. *Goon,* he thought. *Christ.* He didn't know from wrestling but he still couldn't quite fathom why a certain contingent of women would find professional wrestlers attractive. They were mostly losers, actually, guys who couldn't cut it in genuine professional sports. They were little more than circus clowns putting on a human-cannon show. *What's the big deal with wrestlers?* Straker wondered. He lit a cigarette, to ponder these things, when his office door clicked open and in walked Collier, the deputy chief.

Collier had reddish-blond hair that looked fake. And a hardass gleam in his eyes that didn't.

"Hey, DC," Straker said. "I was just about to come by your office. Got a big lead on the Bilks murder."

"Oh yeah? Well it gets a whole lot better. The Sheriff up in Crick City found a mass grave he thinks connects to this case. Twelve bodies, all male in their twenties or thirties; same m.o. with some cute variations, hands, feet, and eyes gone; and get this, their tools are gone. The M.E. said it looks like they were bitten off! They'd all been and I quote 'rectally traumatized.' I'd say this Goon fucker is swinging both ways now."

**44**

"What connects this to our case?" Straker asked feeling suddenly queasy. *Bit their cocks off?* It hurt just to think about it.

"They were able to ID one guy, a big wrestling fan, had a Armageddon Riders logo tattooed on his shoulder. The friend that confirmed the ID said he was at wrestling matches whenever possible trying to get lucky with one of the lady wrestlers or valets."

Straker tapped an ash.

"You're going to have to go undercover on this one, and we've got you some help, a reporter who specializes in pro wrestling coverage."

A reporter? Straker peered at his boss. "Why a reporter—"

"The people you have to get close to are like carnies or gypsies. They practically have their own language. You need someone who knows the game or you'll just be wasting your time." Collier held a sheet of paper. "Just read this and get ready. And *don't* fuck up. Last thing I need is one of my people stepping on his dick in front of the press."

Collier slapped the report down. *Real nice guy.* Straker squinted and read the report:

PAGE ONE OF ONE PAGE
FM: ROANOKE OBSERVER
TO: HQ STATE POLICE VIOLENT CRIMES UNIT
RE: SPECIAL ASSIGNMENT M. PIERCE

Expect arrival of M. Pierce, Special Sports/Entertaiment Columnist Roanoke Observer. Pierce has an extensive background in the field of professional wrestling and has been instructed to provide assistance in any way possible to further your investigation.

L.C. Taylor, Assignment Editor

Straker frowned up at his immediate supervisor. "Come on, DC, they're sending some chump to get a story and fuck things up in the process."

"Yeah. Probably some goddamn whiskey-swilling, cigar-smoking, plaid-jacketed, fat-assed, typewriter jockey. But we gotta live with it."

A shadow crossed the office. Both Collier and Straker turned and stared at the figure who entered: A tall, beautiful blonde in a smart business suit. *Christ Almighty,* Straker mused. *She's absolutely gorgeous...*

"Who are you?" Collier demanded.

"I'm the fat-assed typewriter jockey—I'm sorry I didn't wear plaid today," the woman said. "Melinda Pierce, Sports Columnist."

# PART TWO

She sat primly opposite Straker's desk. 38-24-36, hair shiny as white silk, noon-blue eyes. She tapped notes into a subnotebook computer on her lap. Coltish calves stemmed from a nice pleated, floral skirt; her bosom more than amply filled the lace-trimmed summer-weight blouse, linen-white with simple floral prints. Her face, like a mature model's, bore no signs of make-up, and no signs of anything but a strict, business demeanor. Straker, at 38, had long since forgotten the definition of "automatic erection"; nevertheless, that's what burgeoned in his pants as he tried to beat this stunning distraction and project at least some facsimile of professionalism.

"...seven females that we know of, all but one unidentified, and the twelve guys they dug up outside of Crick City," she was saying. "And I suppose you're curious as to why my paper sent me here? Your boss and mine are old college buddies; he called looking for someone who knew the wrestling game, and here I am."

"Huh?" Straker said.

"The fact is, you have no chance getting close to these people without my help, and this could be the story of the year. And you needn't worry that I'll screw things up for you, I can take care of myself and I know most of these guys real well."

"Huh?" Straker said.

"I'm merely here to assist you in bringing this rash of crimes to resolution."

"Uh, yeah," Straker said.

She set the laptop up on the desk and crossed her legs. Powder blush stockings, slingback white-leather shoes with bronze-hued tips. Her foot tossed unconsciously as she shuffled through some papers.

"I've been on this case for about a month already…" Her blue eyes darted up. "Captain Straker? Are you listening?"

"Uh, oh yes. I was, uh, contemplating the various points of the case."

The most subtle of smirks, then she continued, "As I was saying, I've been working the case in a clandestine capacity for about a month, but my efforts have been fairly futile thus far."

"Clan…destine?"

"An undercover capacity, Captain. All of the victims were what a professional colloquialism refers to as—"

"Ringrats," Straker said in a fog. All he could do was look at her, his erection pulsing.

Her expression focused. "Yes. How did you know that?"

Her legs, her thighs, her hips. The trim waist, the lines of her hips in the skirt, the packed bosom. *Fuck,* he thought dismally. *She's the most beautiful woman I've ever seen in my fuckin' life!* "Uh, oh, yeah. My technical services chief ID'd the seventh body—Susan Bilks. So I interviewed her roommate. It seems that Bilks was hung up on pro wrestlers for some reason. She, you know, got together with them on a regular basis."

"It's called particularized transitive erotomanic behavior," she said. "A groupie phenomenon, which is actually quite apparent in an array of professional circles. For whatever reason, certain women become maniacally attracted to men in a specified occupational field: writers, athletes, rock stars, and in this case, professional wrestlers. And I have reason to believe that a professional wrestler is responsible for all of the murders, a wrestler named—"

"Goon," Straker said.

Another focused glance. "That's uncanny, Captain Straker. How did you determine that?"

Her legs, her thighs, her hips… "Uh, oh, I read Bilks' diary."

"A diary? That's fantastic. How did you manage to get her diary?"

*You don't want to know.* Straker's stomach flipped. The diary. The visual images of what he'd had to do to get it seemed like jumpcuts of some bizarre organic nightmare. Miss Wilcox had spread her run-down-by-a-Mack-Truck body out on the trailer floor, unhesitant in her withered nakedness. Cunnilingus, of course, had been her first request, and her fingers had bared the open sump of her sex before Straker's flinching face, digging into it as though it were a plop of Alpo. With hair around it. "Lick it," she breathily ordered, and when Straker did, the flavor made him think of what a meld of ground pork and anchovies might taste like after it had sufficiently spoiled. The flattened breasts flopped to her armpits as the splayed hips sensitively fidgeted. "Now fuck it," she ordered. "Dump a great big hot *fuck* in that pussy, you big handsome fucker you!" It was only sheer reflex that permitted erection at all, Straker's unquenched-for-years libido rising to a potential reproductive occasion. When he slid his penis into that gasping vaginal mess, he was grateful that forced images of a stacked, blond babysitter named Wendy allowed him to empty his vesicles rather quickly. When he withdrew, there came a wet squish, like someone rowing a stick through spaghetti. "Oh, shit, yes! That's just what I needed, a pussyful of cum." And she'd made him do it all one more time before she'd given him the diary, her on top the second time, her popped bags for breasts slapping his face. "Give me another nut!" she profaned. "Squirt that hot cum all the way up there, you fucker!" *What am I?* Straker pondered. *A sperm vendor?* The second trip had taken a bit longer as that sloppy vagina gulped him. More squishy sounds, like people scarfing scrambled eggs, abounded until he was finally able to aspirate his semen yet again. Afterward, she gave him the diary, then lay sated on the rag-tag couch, playing with the leakage at the raw gulf, then sucking it off her fingers. "Come back and see me sometime," she said and winked. *Doubtful,* Straker thought.

The recollection clashed, though, with what he was looking at right now: Melinda Pierce, a brick shithouse in a $400 dress. Bits of questions, however, did manage to surface over his muse of dreamy lust.

"How did you know about this guy Goon?"

"Confidential," she said. "I've been watching him for a while."

"So does he have a record?."

"Not that anyone can find."

"Then what's his professional history"

"No one knows. His manager, Felander, just showed up with him last year. He'd been managing after he blew his knee and dropped out of the Armageddon Riders. With his charisma he was one of the top

managers within a couple of months, started managing his old crony Dare and the Fabulous Ghoula. Then about a year ago he drops the two biggest names in the region and starts working with a mid-card heel. It doesn't make a lot of sense financially. Felander, Dare, Ruger, and Kevin the Druid were the top of the wrestling profession for almost a decade. And that's another thing—The Druid."

Hadn't Traci Wilcox mentioned that name? *Yes.* "According to her room-mate, Susan Bilks got…picked up by Kevin the Druid once."

"The Druid was well-known for being a ring-rat addict. He and Felander were good friends. Kevin's gimmick was a satanic schtick; he'd wear black capes and upside-down crosses in the ring. It worked for years. But it seems like the same time Goon showed up, Kevin the Druid disappeared. And I mean disappeared without a trace. No one's seen him since."

*Interesting,* Straker thought. *But what's even more interesting are her perfect giant state-of-the-art tits that I'd give a year's pay just to suck for one second.* The most ludicrous fantasy bloomed: They were married, she was pregnant, lactating. *Yeah, man, I'd be sucking on those tits so much there'd be no milk left for the kid.*

"Anyway, all of a sudden Felander drops Dare, Ruger, and Ghoula, the only really bi names in the fed."

Straker shook himself, trying to get his mind off those breasts. "How old is Goon? What's he look like? Where's he from?"

"It's more of eliminating where he's not from, there's no record of him having an amateur career, and a guy that size would've have gotten some press, and he's not from any of the training schools. The first thing I did some months ago was check with Barry Sharpe at the Ogre Academy and Stew Hartley in Canada and they'd never heard of him. He must be some gym-rat that Felander met somewhere, but what I can't figure out is how he became the caliber of worker he is with only a couple of months training."

When she took a breath, her bosom gently heaved. Straker felt dizzy, mad with breast-lust. *Yeah, I'd like to milk 'em, milk 'em into a big bucket and drown myself in the milk. What a way to go.* He had to bite the inside of his cheek just to re-focus. "All right. You said you've been working on the case in an undercover capacity. How?"

"How do you think?" she casually replied. "I've been posing as a ringrat."

⊛ — ⊛ — ⊛

"I guess the best place to start," Melinda Pierce said behind the wheel of her heather-green Ford Taurus, "is with the preliminary structure of professional wrestling at large. I take it you're not a wrestling fan, Captain?"

Straker kept shifting the position of his ass in the passenger seat, and tried his best to not seem obvious in the way he covered his lap with his hand. Before they'd left HQ, he'd had no choice but to excuse himself. "Quick stop to the little boy's room," he gushed. "Be right back." Whereupon he paranoically stepped up to the urinal, cast quick glances over each shoulder, then sprang his erection out and quickly masturbated. He felt silly and ashamed. *What the hell is wrong with me? I see a hot-looking woman and suddenly I'm running off to the bathroom to beat my meat like some teenager!* The draining that Miss Wilcox and her bologna vagina had inflicted didn't leave much left; nevertheless, in his keen excitement, Straker only needed a quick series of shucks to coax an orgasm which left him rubber-kneed. Brow sweating, he looked down and saw the white string of his reproductive milk dangling from the egress of his penis like a piece of vermicelli. He flapped it off, stuffed said penis back into his pants, and rushed out to rejoin Melinda Pierce of the Roanoke Observer. He knew he was being paranoid, but she seemed to smile oh-so-subtly when he returned. Moments later, they were in her car and heading down Main Street. Destination unknown.

Straker replied, hips flinching, "Un, no, Ms. Pierce. I'm not a wrestling fan. Sometimes I see it on TV but only when I'm changing stations. What? We're talking Hunk Hargan, Hunkamania, stuff like that? And what's that other guy's name with all the paint all over his face. Poison?"

"Venom, Captain, and, no, we are not talking about that echelon of professional wrestling. Those are the big feds."

"Feds?"

"Federations. Think of them as the biggest and most profitable pro wrestling organizations. These guys wrestle five or six nights a week, and are frequently on national television. They make lots of money given the exposure. But Goon doesn't wrestle for either of the big feds. He wrestles for DSWC—that's the Deep South Wrestling Conference. It's a regional conference, small-time compared to WWF and WCW. Think of it as the difference between the minor leagues and the major league. It's a much smaller draw, but it's still very consistent."

Straker pretended to be listening, looking at those plush spread thighs laying in the driver's seat, the elegant hands holding the wheel, the plenteous bosom riding in the sheer white floral-print blouse. "So I guess this guy Goon is a light-weight," Straker managed. He grit his teeth imperceptibly, feeling the flare of another erection.

"Quite the contrary. Goon is the best wrestler in the world."

Straker blinked. "If he's so good, then how come he's not working for the 'big feds'?"

"Because he doesn't want to. In fact, his manager had turned down repeated contracts with WWF and WCW for many times the amount of money that Goon's making now. Kind of like a small-town cop turning down repeated offers with state and/or county PDs."

"That doesn't make any sense," Straker pointed out, feeling his gorged corona now nudging the bottom of his hiding hand. He felt tempted to give it a squeeze. "Nobody turns down bigger money."

"Goon does," she said. "And I'll tell you why. In a fed as small as DSWC, Goon isn't subject to the widespread exposure of television and nation-wide cards."

"Cards?"

"A card, Captain, is an ensemble of wrestling matches. And another thing of note is this: Goon's got the ultimate gimmick."

"Gimmick?"

"You can think of a 'gimmick' as a 'set' in a movie or a persona. A 'work' is the script. The conclusion of each match is predetermined by the promoters. The 'bookers' are essentially the people who create and maintain the characterization of the fed. Who's rivaling who, who's turning bad, who's turning good, etc. It's a storyline, which the fans follow as diligently as Star Trek fans follow *Voyager* and *Deep Space Nine* and all that. And Goon's the ultimate heel."

Straker grit his teeth again. Just looking at those luscious legs made him want to come in his pants. "Heel?" he questioned.

"Professional nomenclature. Heels are bad guys, faces are good guys. And pro wrestling perpetuates via the proliferation of the ongoing rivalries that exist between faces and heels. Same as the rivalry, for instance, between the Redskins and the Cowboys, or, more appropriately, the rivalry between the Roman gladiators and the armed slaves in the arena. That's all wrestling is, Captain. They're the Gladiators of modern civilization."

Straker knew that if he so much as brushed his crotch with his hand, he'd come, envisioning her. He'd mess his pants, indeed, like a torqued-up teen eyeing the hot biology teacher or one of the cheerleaders jumping up like a flying human wishbone on the sidelines. *I need to come again,* he dismally thought. *I can't fucking stand this!*

"But the Gladiators were real," he finally was able to get back on track. "Wrestling isn't. Everyone knows it's fake."

"It's not as fake as you think, Captain," she said, and then unconsciously brushed her hand flat against her right thigh. Straker nearly creamed his shorts, nearly groaned at the image.

"It's true, most of these guys are athletes who weren't good enough to make it in legitimate professional sports. Leon Black, aka Big Dan Tater, got cut from the L.A. Rams, Leapin' Leonard got cut from the Bengals, Don Clemmens got cut from the Lions. Derrick Lotts was a college football quarterback, a starter, who got kicked out of pro camp on the second day, and Venom tried out with four minor league baseball teams and never got a hit. So, yes, these guys are what pro sports spat out, but they're still unique athletes in their own way. You say wrestling's fake? Well, in a sense, it is, but when a wrestler jumps off the top rope, launches himself ten feet into the air, and lands on his opponent, it is indeed a prearranged work, but that man is still leaping ten feet into the air and landing on a human being. These guys piledrive each other's heads on the cement ring curtain, but if you don't know what you're doing, you wind up with a broken neck, and that instance has happened to several wrestlers. Several wrestlers have had their ears shorn off by a make involves getting their heads stuck in the ring ropes. Pro wrestlers blow out their knees at a much higher rate than pro running backs. Concussions abound, Achilles tendons snap like draw-strings, and wrestlers have suffered more broken bones than the ath-letes of any other professional sport. It's something to consider before you scoff completely at wrestling as a joke. These men are high-tuned athletes—they have to be in order to circumvent serious injury any given night of the week. Which leads us back to Goon."

"Goon," Straker said, as if to seem as though he were being atten-tive. His only real attentiveness, however, was sighted on Melinda Pierce's 38D breasts. In his mind, he saw his face buried between them, his eyes crossed in bliss.

"Even in DSWC, Goon has refused major heel slots that would earn him two or three times the money he makes now. He's the hottest prop-erty in the fed. Goon works as the ultimate hardcore, whenever he wrestles the fans know they're going to see someone do heavy juice. Felander books all the finishes and no one objects. Why? Because he can take punishment like no other. Chairs, tables, two-by-fours, etc. have all been broken over Goon's head more times than you've taken that shirt to the cleaners."

*I'm gonna have to take these shorts to the cleaners in about one minute,* Straker thought. "Juice? Aren't the chairs, tables, and two-by-fours all fake?"

"That's where you're wrong, Captain. That stuff's all the real McCoy—it has to be because it's all in proximity to fans. Juice is real blood, not the capsules that actors use; some wrestlers carry little razor blades to open up cuts above the hairline, Goon does what they call 'hardway juice,' he actually has the other wrestler bust him open with something. Quite regularly, you'll see Goon jump off the top rope, do a somersault, and land on his back on the cement ring skirt. I suppose you're going to tell me it's phony cement?"

Straker shrugged. His balls felt large as Roma tomatoes now, filling up with enough sperm cells to populate entire planets. "I don't know. I probably know as much about professional wrestling as you know about the Battle of Hastings."

"October 14th, A.D. 1066, King Harold Godwin attempted to defend the island of Angle-land against the forces of William of Normandy on a coastal rise called Senlac Hill, otherwise known as

Hastings. Three Norman assaults failed but a fourth succeeded after Harold was killed by a stray Norman arrow which hit him in the eye, but that's beside the point, Captain. The fact remains, these men, professional wrestlers, must remain in extraordinary condition in order to do what they do night after night without crippling or killing themselves. And Goon is the best of the best. You'll see, Captain. You'll see tonight."

*Jesus Christ I've got to come,* Straker thought. His dick felt like a yard hose about to split from too much pressure. *I can't even be in the same car with this piece of work without wanting to spew all over myself.*

His thoughts drifted back. "What? What do you mean, tonight?"

"We're going to a wrestling match tonight," she said. "And you and I are both going undercover."

✵ — ✵ — ✵

Her keys jingled at the end of a silver judo stick when she let them into the motel.

"I need to use your bathroom," Straker said.

"Sure. Right in there."

Straker traipsed away, closed the door behind him. Two seconds later, his erect penis was out, and he was shucking it like an ear of corn. *Aw, fuck! There's just something about her,* he thought. *I just...can't... help it...* About ten jerks did the trick, and out it came, his forth orgasm of the day and another piece of vermicelli relegated to the toilet. They just kept getting better, thinking about her, and that's what he didn't get. Straker had long since dismissed his sex drive as fairly dead once he'd reached thirty. He didn't give a shit anymore, and that was fine—he had better things to occupy his mind than sex. Additionally, he saw attractive women all the time, and didn't flinch...

But Melinda Pierce was quite a bit more than merely attractive.

She was the woman of his dreams. She was sex incarnate. She was a vision equal to that which launched a thousand ships in the Trojan War. Straker sighed, rubbing the last drop of semen with his index finger against the cringing glans. The sensation drove him to his tiptoes, and when he imagined Melinda Pierce doing the same, only with her tongue, and he was half hard again even before he got it back into his pants.

He rushed back out, collecting himself. She'd rented a cheap motel room off Route 154, with Observer funds no doubt. "Here are the tickets," she said when he emerged and nearly hit the floor. She'd kicked her shoes off, extending her long legs across the couch, and she'd removed her blouse to reveal the exorbitant breasts satcheled perfectly in a tan-lace bra.

"What's the matter? You've never seen a woman in a bra before?"

"I—" And that was all Straker could manage. Her hand reached out, holding tickets. Straker's cock thumped to something close to full hardness again when he took them. Idly, and nearly dizzy, he read:

### SALLEE COUNTY CIVIC CENTER, 7:00 P.M.
### OPEN SEATING. DEEP SOUTH WRESTLING CONFERENCE
### REGIONAL SUMMER RUMBLE.

"Great," Straker said dully. "I can't wait."

"Goon's on the card, grappling against Slick Dare."

"Great." *I would pay anything,* he thought. *I would sell my soul just to rub my dick against one of those tits for one second. Then I could die, and I'd be fulfilled.* The image of those bra'd breasts socked him in the eyes. The sleek lounging legs stretched out to the arm of the couch. Age-old high school cliche's came to mind: *I'd gargle with her piss...and ask for more. I'd eat a mile of her shit just to see where it came from. If she was fucking dead, I'd dig her up and marry her...*

"Are you all right?"

Straker's eyes snapped open. He'd been musing again, about her. "Yeah, uh, sure. I'm fine."

"You were standing there kind of fidgeting your hips."

*That's because my dick's hard again, and it got stuck in the trapdoor of my shorts.* "Just a...cold chill."

She inclined up, then rose and grabbed a bag off the motel desk. "Put these on, you need to look the part."

Straker peered into the bag: jeans, sneakers, a black t-shirt with the Armageddon Riders logo. "The part for what?"

"Tonight we're going to this card. I'm going as a ringrat, and you're going as a fan. You can't expect to gain any credibility going to a wrestling match dressed in a suit that makes you look like Jack Webb."

Straker recoiled. "There's nothing wrong with this suit. It cost two hundred bucks."

"Wow. Big spender. I'll bet Ward's loves you. Listen, Captain, you can't walk into a wrestling match wearing a suit. You'll stick out like a sore thumb. So why don't you get dressed now, and I'll go take a quick shower before I get into my ringrat gear."

"Yeah, sure."

She sashayed off into the bathroom, pushed the door shut behind her. Then he heard the hiss of the shower crank on and almost lost it. It was the image...

Her.

In there.

Taking her clothes off and stepping into the shower, all shiny and perfect and nude.

Straker couldn't help it. He whipped it out and began masturbating over the plastic, bag-lined wastebasket.

*Aw, fuck, aw, fuck*— His climax spasmed; he nearly fell down. *If Collier could see me now,* he thought, wringing out his cock over the garbage can. His sperm plopped to the bottom. Then he sluggishly disrobed and put on the clothes in the bag.

*I look like a horse's ass,* he thought, appraising himself in the motel mirror. Brand-new dark-denim Lee jeans fit so tight he couldn't even fasten the brass button. He pulled the black t-shirt out over his waist and frowned more deeply. The shirt read ARMAGEDDON RIDERS! KICKIN' ASS AND NOT TAKIN' NAMES! On the front with the DSWC logo on the back. Just what some ignorant cracker would wear on a Saturday night out, basic attire for hard-liquor and handgun night. Hard as he may have been trying to quit, he sat down on the couch, and listlessly lit a cigarette. *I'm undercover with the woman of my dreams, and I'm wearing a fuckin' wrestling shirt.* If any of his ex-girlfriends could see this, they'd laugh to wake the dead.

"Close your eyes," came her muffled voice.

Stifled, Straker closed them. "All right."

He heard her come out of the bathroom, bringing with her a scent of herbal soap. Then he heard clothes sliding against skin, and imagined her dressing; an unconscious reflex nearly caused him to squeeze his crotch, but he repressed the impulse. *Jesus,* he thought. *If she knew I've jerked off three times since meeting her—twice right in this motel room—I'd have to kill myself.*

"Okay. Open."

Straker opened his eyes and nearly shit and came in his pants simultaneously. She stood there with her back towards him, wearing nothing but a tight denim skirt whose hem barely reached the bottom of her buttocks. She was bare up top, cradling her breasts in her hands.

"Pass me that pink halter over there, will you?"

Straker grabbed the halter on the dresser, draped it over her shoulder. It was all he could do not to do a rebel yell when she raised her arms and slipped herself into it. Only a second, true, but in that second Straker stared at sideshots of both breasts from behind. And nearly collapsed.

"Zip me now, okay?"

She leaned slightly forward and Straker caught what she meant. The back of that tight denim skirt—it had a zipper in back.

Straker's finger's shook like an alcoholic with the DTs; eventually he grasped the tiny metal tab, caught his breath, then pulled it up with a rasp.

"Thanks," she said and turned. The haltered breasts blared at him. Hard City yet again. "One more thing," she requested. "I need you to do my toes."

Oblivious, Straker only fought not to stare, and didn't do much of a job. His own jeans were so tight, his cock felt like a snake in a closing crevice. Only in the most nebulous fog did he recall what she said: *I need you to do my—*

"My toes," she repeated, pulilng up a chair to face the couch. "While I do my nails." She placed her hands on his shoulder and pushed him down into the chair, then sat down herself.

"I—," he said.

She placed her bare feet right smack dab in his lap. Zombiefied now, all he could do was look. Her nude feet flexed very close to his groin—

even her feet were perfect—but when he noticed her blue-painted toe-nails, he could only think to say, "Your toes are already done."

"No they're not. I'm posing as a ringrat. That means I've got to look as tacky as possible. Decals, Captain." Then she handed him a strip of paper, adhered to which were a dozen tiny silver decals of falling stars. She held a similar strip and daintily affixed each decal to her finger-nails. Straker doddered, peeled each one off and clumsily affixed them to her veneered toenails.

"Perfect," she appraised when they were both done. She alternately glanced first at her fingernails, then her toenails. *I need to beat off again,* Straker thought. *Bad.* Then she briskly rose, and in doing so accidentally brushed one of her heels across his crotch.

*Shit!*

"Sorry," she said.

One more brush like that and he'd have come again. He winced, ris-ing, trying to hide his fifth erection of the day. "All right, I guess we can go to this wrestling match now."

The pause hung in the air. She looked at him forlornly, her lips pursed. "Listen, Captain, I can tell something's wrong, and I think I know what it is."

Straker had to sort the statement; he had to struggle against his lust. "What? There's nothing wrong."

"Yes, there is, Captain. It seems that you're incredibly attracted to me."

"What, uh, what makes you say that?"

"Well, for one thing," she responded, "you've either had the end of a broomstick in your pants since the minute we met, or you're carrying around a raging erection."

The observation jostled him. All he could do was lie. "That's ridicu-lous. You don't know what you're talking ab—"

"And it seems that you're so attracted to me, you've had to mastur-bate to relive your tensions."

Straker gaped. "I have not!"

She looked scoldingly at him. "Captain. When you used the bath-room, you forgot to flush the toilet. I saw your sperm floating in the water."

Straker's mouth formed an O like a grouper's, but no words came out.

Then she glanced intermittently into the wastebasket. "And it looks like you've done it again right there in the garbage."

Straker could only stare. He could say nothing as his face turned red as a radish.

She patted his shoulder consolingly. "Listen, Captain, I understand. I sometimes have this effect on men, and I apologize. Tell you what I'll do. I'll go wait in the car, and you can masturbate again if you'd like."

Straker nearly threw up as he watched her leave the motel room. Could anything be more embarrassing than this?

The answer was simple: No. Nothing in the world.

Nevertheless, he whipped it out one more time, and masturbated desperately until he was able to deposit yet another string of semen into the bag-lined plastic wastebasket.

*Asshole,* he thought.

✸ — ✸ — ✸

She didn't say a word when he summoned the courage to actually walk out to the car and get in. They rode in silence for at least five minutes, heading for Route 154. Finally, Straker could bare no more of it.

"Listen," he said. "I couldn't help it."

"Oh, don't worry," she said. "Men find me attractive. I know that."

Straker scratched his face. "Well, what about..."

"Yes, Captain?"

"Well, I was just curious. I mean, do, uh, do you find, uh, me attractive?"

"No," she said. She steered down the road, unaffected. Only after a commensurate pause did she add, "But that's not to make you feel inadequate, Captain. I'm sure a good many women are sufficiently attracted to you. It's just that I'm not one of them. It's not an insult, you know."

"Sure," Straker said. But what could he expect her to say? 38 now, growing a pot and losing his hair in back. He hadn't lifted a weight in ten years, and the last time he'd had a suntan, Carter was in office. *I'm a pud,* he condemned himself. *I'm an blithering idiot. I just let the most desirable woman in the world catch me beating off...*

"You're not, uh—you know—you're not like going to, uh, tell anyone are you?"

She smiled as she drove. "Of course not, Captain. That's not really the sort of thing I'd want to have put in the case file. And I don't know what you're so embarrassed about. Masturbation is a normal, healthy mode of sexual release. Everyone masturbates, Captain. *I* masturbate."

His gaze roved dismally out the window. "Oh yeah? How often?"

"Oh, I don't know. Periodically."

Periodically. That probably didn't mean four times in little more than an hour. He'd really done it this time; humiliation could not be more complete than this. When had the last time been? Two months ago? No, more like three or four. And today's earlier shenanigans with Traci Wilcox had been his first intercourse in over a year. It was Melinda Pierce's fault, he knew. It was her presence that had revived the long forgotten sex drive. She was the bolt of lightning that could resurrect the dead.

There seemed little point now in preserving any professional acumen. She'd caught him beating off, for Christ's sake! "Are you married?" he asked.

"Oh, no. My job is my priority," she informed him, steering down the road. "You're a cop, you know what I mean."

At least that much was true. "Yeah, but I'm sure you've got a boyfriend."

"Nope. Not interested."

This seemed unfathomable. As good-looking as she was? She could walk into any New York modeling agency and leave with a contract. She could be in movies or tv. *She could be anything,* he realized. *But she's chosen to be a reporter instead, and she accepts the sacrifices.* Straker had accepted those same sacrifices but more by default than anything less. Yet her resolve was crystal clear.

"Let me ask you something," he said, taking the thought a step further. "You've gone undercover as a ringrat. It's the same as a narc, in a way. You lose your credibility when it gets down to the wire, don't you?"

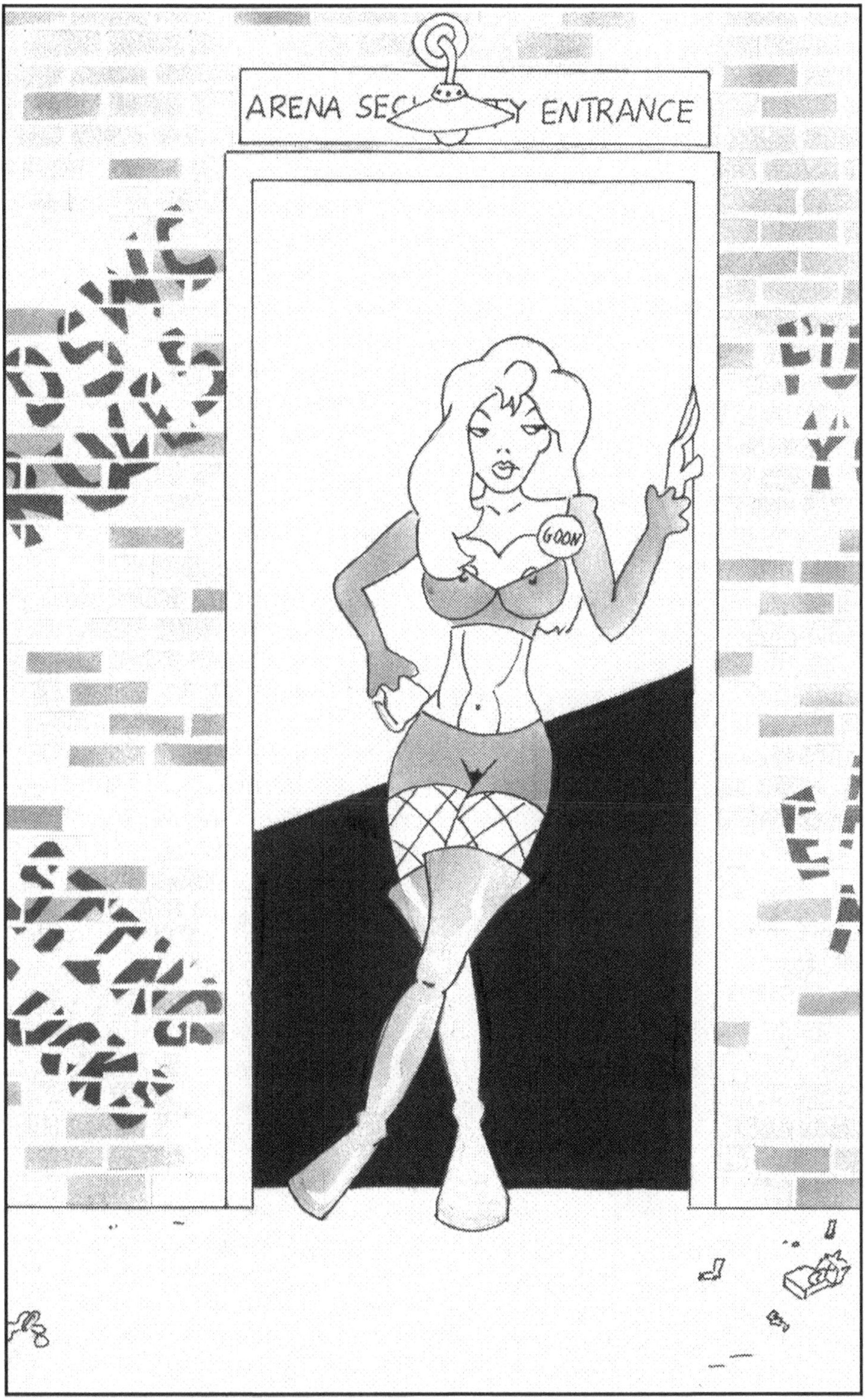
ARENA SEC
Y ENTRANCE
GOON

She glanced confused at him. "What do you mean?"

"I mean, if a narc is posing as a dopehead, his credibility only lasts as long as it takes for someone to wonder why he's never been seen actually taking drugs."

"Oh, I get it. And you want to know how I can maintain the premise of being a ringrat without really having sex with wrestlers."

"Yeah."

"That's not a problem, Captain. I've been able to successfully infiltrate the local ringrat community because I *do* have sex with wrestlers."

Straker's neck nearly snapped when he jerked his gaze to her. "You're kidding me, right?"

"No. And what's so odd about that? We're pros, Captain. We do what we need to do to get the job done, period. Even if it means we have to do things that would otherwise be considered a breech of professional conduct."

Straker was suddenly riled. "You mean you actually, you-you-you...*get it on* with those guys?"

"Of course. I have to. Otherwise I'd have no undercover credibility at all. My job is to get the real story on Goon. I can't do that unless I can get close to him, and I can't get close to him unless I'm believable as a ringrat. Goon has a vulnerability; I'll find that vulnerability by getting to his manager, and I know I'll eventually get to his manager by—pardon the word—fucking the right grappler."

This was incredulous. Was she serious? Straker could tell, by her poise, her gestures, and the tone of her voice that she meant every word of it.

Then she continued, "And don't tell me you've never done anything technically unethical in order to do your job more effectively."

Straker bumbled, was about to object, but then fell silent. *She's right,* he realized. Just this morning he'd had sex—twice—in order to obtain Susan Bilks' diary. So he could hardly criticize Melinda Pierce for having sex with wrestlers in order to do her job.

"It's just...kind of shocking is all," he eventually remarked.

Then she looked him dead in the eye. "Goon has raped, mutilated, and murdered at least nineteen people that we know of, Captain. I will do anything to stop him. Anything."

Straker stared at the poison in her eyes. *You know something?* he thought. *She means it.*

⊛ — ⊛ — ⊛

The bell clanged. Sallee County Civic Center, little more than a high school gymnasium, had packed in over a thousand people. Straker was taken aback by the sight of the crowd: mostly rednecks, mostly adults. Cheering, waving signs, wearing shirts and caps emblazoned with the likenesses of their favorite "grapplers." Straker and Melinda never went to their seats; instead they stood by the railed ring entrance along with about a hundred other people, mostly women dressed similarly to Melinda.

Ringrats.

"How come we're not going to our seats?" he asked over the din. Right now, in the ring, Terri Strong and the Fabulous Ghoula were trading combinations on the mat.

"The rats generally hang by the locker room access for the whole show," she said, her eyes glued to the ring. "The idea is to catch the eye of a grappler as he's coming out, then try to snag him later."

It made sense and, frankly, Straker wasn't too keen to sit anywhere near the ring. Everytime a wrestler was slapped, drop-kicked, or body-slammed, a rain of sweat sprayed the crowd.

But this current match fascinated him. Two women. "Wow. Lady wrestlers." Ghoula, obviously the heel, was being tossed around the ring like a sack of packing curls, not an easy feat, he didn't imagine, because the woman probably weighted 300 pounds. Strong, on the other hand, in spite of a gymnast's arms, was ravishingly attractive.

"They pepper the cards with some of the bigger name females," Melinda said. "The fans love to see women fight."

Strong rode Ghoula across the ring in a headlock, but suddenly the obese woman fell to the mat, sending Strong's head into the ringpost. And when Strong groggily rose, her face shone with blood.

"Gross," Straker observed.

"Kill her!" Melinda shouted, her breasts bobbling as she rose to her tip toes. Now Ghoula was biting Terri Strong's face as she squirmed on the canvas, her muscular legs kicking amid a sound like thunder. Ghoula cracked out an evil chuckle, her blubber jiggling in black tights, her grin pocked by missing teeth. *She is the most disgusting human being I've ever seen,* Straker affirmed to himself, but Melinda, as though reading his thoughts, smiled uncharacteristically and said, "How'd you like a roll in the hay with her?"

"No thanks," Straker said, queasy at the image. *I'd sooner put a gun to my head.*

Ghoula's fat visibly tremored as she dragged Strong to her feet, then grasped her head between her palms, pressing, pressing. The effect made it appear as though she was squeezing blood out of Strong's face. "This is a lot more violent than I thought," Straker observed, his stomach knotting. "But I guess it's nothing more than the power of suggestion, you know, the fake blood and all."

"It's not fake," she told him.

"Come on."

"Strong bladed herself when she had the headlock on Ghoula. Remember, the more blood the bigger the draw."

Strong had just taken a drop-kick at Ghoula's head, the larger woman ducked under the kick and using her shoulder heaved her opponent over the top rope to the floor. The crowd was really into it, with a chant of "You fucked up! You fucked up!" being shouted at the prone girl who was being further humiliated by a rain of popcorn, candy wrappers, and other soft-drink cups as she groggily got to her feet.

"This is a real hard-core crowd here, she missed her move, she was supposed to catch the top rope and pull herself back into the ring while Ghoula had her back turned. These fans are pretty unforgiving when someone screws up."

"So the blood was a 'work' but falling on the floor was an accident?"

"You're catching on, Captain."

Straker didn't know if he believed it, but one thing he did believe was there were some great-looking women around the entrance aisle. All around them, and on the other side of the railed aisle, ringrats congregated as a shrieking mass: tackily dressed, painted up with more makeup than a French whore, but beautiful nonetheless. "This is incredible," Straker went on. "These women aren't dogs—they're gorgeous. What the hell do they see in a bunch of goddamn wrestlers?"

"It's a sexual psychology, Captain. Why is it okay for men to lust, but not women? It's the Blonde Bimbo Syndrome in reverse. Ringrats are simply playing a fantasy role. You don't see any kids here; rats aren't like teeny-bopper rock star groupies. They're adult women who've grown disgusted with the sexual exploitation of our society. So they dress up and come to the ring so they can be sluts for a night. They regard wrestlers as nothing more than pieces of sexual meat to be used in order to fulfill their own fantasies. Male-dominated society has been sexually exploiting women for the last fifty centuries. Well, women become ringrats so they can do a little exploitation of their own. Here, the *wrestlers* are the bimbos."

An interesting extrapolation, but Straker still didn't quite get it. These guys were dopes.

"Don't be such a hopeless romantic, Captain. Women are sick of double-standards. If men can be promiscuous, so can we."

"You almost sound like you're one of them," Straker pointed out. "A real ringrat."

She casually hitched up her halter. "Perhaps, in part, I am."

*Jesus.* She certainly was interesting, but Straker, oblivious to his own double-standards, couldn't keep his eyes off her. Every so often she'd lean forward against the rail, giving him a glimpse of devil-red panties. The firm, heavy breasts swayed in the top as she cheered, and two or three times her rump accidentally brushed his groin. Straker winced in anguish, his penis hard again.

"Watch the finish," she said. "Strong will duck and throw Ghoula into the ringpost. Then Ghoula'll turn and throw a ball of fire right into Strong's face."

Straker tried to concentrate over the cacophony, then winced as if slapped when The Fabulous Ghoula whipped around and did exactly what Melinda had predicted. There was a loud *pop!* Then a radiating, smoky sphere of flame seemed to leap from her hand into Strong's face. Strong went down, flailing in phony agony. Bells clattered, and then the ref waved his arms and disqualified Ghoula. The crowd exploded.

"Wow," Straker said dumbly. "How'd she do that?"

"A flashpot, that's all. The heat dissipates almost immediately."

Some patrons were actually in tears as Strong was carried off on a stretcher, her hands clenched to her face. Then Ghoula jumped down onto the ring skirt and kicked the stretcher over. A few kicks to Strong's head, then Ghoula strutted off, cackling like a witch as fans booed, threw cups at her, hurled invectives.

When she strode down the railed aisle toward the locker room, however, she took one look at Straker and stopped. "Looks like this is your lucky day," Melinda whispered. *Oh, no,* Straker fretted. He could smell the obese woman as she approached, a fetor like dirty musk. Then she stepped right up to him, cut a sly, gap-toothed grin, and winked.

"Hey, sweetcakes," she said.

"You talkin' to me?" Straker blundered.

Unabashed she pressed her sweaty, mat-stinky hand against his crotch, gave a squeeze.

"This package for me, sweetcakes?"

Straker stared, appalled. Her malodor reamed his sinuses. She gave his crotch another shameless squeeze. "Yeah, sweetcakes. I like this package. Meet me at the bar later and I'll unwrap it for ya."

Then she threw her head back, guffawed, and strode away, her sheath of fat trembling like jello.

"I think I'm gonna be sick," Straker moaned.

But Melinda excitedly grabbed his arm. "This is perfect! What a lucky break!"

"What are you talking about?"

Melinda's breath warmed his ear as she whispered. "Are you blind? She's got the hots for you! She thinks you're a male ringrat."

"Yeah, well, she can think again."

"Captain, this is an ideal opportunity for you to go undercover just like me. You can get together with her later—"

Straker's jaw dropped. "Not in this lifetime," he assured her. "You've got to be out of your mind if you think I'd—"

Her glare of disapproval severed the words. "What's the matter, Captain? Not willing to go the course for the sake of the case?"

"No," Straker said.

"Don't have what it takes to do the job right?"

"No," Straker said. "I'm not going to 'get together' with that obese, unwashed female blimp. And, anyway, she's got nothing to do with Goon. There's no information I could worm out of her that would be relevant to this investigation."

"That's where you're dead wrong, Captain." She pulled him closer, whispered more fervently. "Goon's manager used to be her manager. If you slept with her, you could pump her for all kinds of information."

Straker couldn't believe what she was proposing. "Well you can forget that 'cos it ain't gonna happen."

Her pursed lips told all. "I guess I was right about you. Won't go the extra mile to get the job done."

"Ain't gonna happen," he repeated, determined.

"We'll talk about this later."

"No. We won't. 'Cos it ain't gonna happen." Her silence unsettled him but he didn't care. What she wanted him to do was clearly absurd, not to mention wholly unethical. But before he could mull it over any further, a great gong sounded, and suddenly some dork in a tux was standing in the middle of the ring with a microphone.

"Ladies and gentlemen, our main event. This is a title match for the DSWC heavyweight championship belt!"

The crowd stirred in frenzy; the arena was actually shaking. Tux went on after another gong. "Entering the ring from your left, from Minneapolis, Minnesota, six-foot-three and weighing in at 243 pounds…"

The gong sounded yet again.

"…12-time World Heavyweight Champion! The styler and profiler! The fourth horseman of the apocalypse! Ladies and gentlemen, the Deep South Wrestling Conference Heavyweight Champion! The Wonder Boy! *Sliiiiiiiiiiick* Dare!"

A spotlight snapped on, illuminating the ring entrance, and there he was. Straker frowned as the arena quaked. Dare stood pompously, fists on hip, draped in a glittering purple robe with a white fur collar. Cropped hair bleached close to snow white, and a California tan. In spite of the age lines in his face, and a web of forehead scars, and in spite of the falseness of all of this, the man seemed to project some kind of aura that affected Straker as genuine. But Straker couldn't voice that, so instead he reverted to sarcasm. "Six three my ass. That guy's five-eleven if he's anything."

"They exaggerate a little. Once they're in the ring, the really do look larger than life. Almost like gods."

*Gods. Gimme a break.*

Melinda seemed keenly focused, staring at this bleached blond icon. Under her breath, she even commented, "I can see why all the ringrats are nuts about him. He's really...hot."

Straker frowned hard. "He looks like a broken-down jalopy. What is he, sixty?"

"He's forty five, but twenty years of bodyslams, suplexes, and dropkicks to the face will wear anybody down. At least Dare's aged with grace."

"Oh, make me puke," Straker countered. "What did he do, dig up Liberace for the robe? Oh, and I love his hair. I hope this guy can write hair bleach off on his taxes. And, Jesus Christ, look at that hammy tin-foil belt."

"Captain Straker," Melinda coyly suggested. "Do I detect a hint of jealousy?"

Straker laughed. "What have I got to be jealous about? That guy's a busted loser."

"Yeah? Well that busted loser has probably made ten million dollars in the last twenty years."

Straker paused and gulped. "You're pulling my leg."

"He's the most successful wrestler of all time. In his heyday he could write his own ticket, he was the biggest draw in the sport."

Straker's face pinched up. *Ten million dollars? These guys make that kind of money for this phony farce?*

"And just wait till you see him in the ring," she added.

Eventually Dare broke from his pretentious stance, then strutted to the ring as the crowd's roar rose. Melinda grabbed Straker's arm again, and he secretly gasped. Just being touched by her, however cursorily, sent a line of prickles up his back...and through his groin.

"What?"

"See that guy there, standing just at the locker room entrance?"

Straker glanced. A big beefy guy in a black shirt, short dark hair and a goatee. "That's Goon?" he questioned.

"No, no, that's Felander, Goon's manager, he used to wrestle as one of the Riders with Dare, and the Druid, and Rex Ruger. He was The Pain Doctor," she whispered. "That's the guy who'll lead us to Goon and the evidence you need to put him away."

Straker didn't get it. He still couldn't reason why they didn't get federal help in to go after Goon directly; after all, everything said this guy was a serial-killer. But now the crowd was in such an uproar, Straker could scarcely hear his thoughts much less dwell on the reason he was here.

The ring announcer's voice jerked Straker's attention back up. Then a wash of heavy-metal guitar riffs, like chainsaws buzzing in unison, cut through the air.

"And tonight's opponent, ladies and gentlemen, entering the ring accompanied by his manager—at six feet seven inches tall and weighing in a 350 pounds! Hailing from parts unknown! *Goooooooooooon!*"

Straker shuddered at the crowd's response: a deafening meld of boos, jeers, and cheers. A shadow which seemed immense lingered at the entrance, and Straker could only stare at its size. But suddenly Melinda's hands were on him again.

"Stand in front of me," she whispered. "I don't want him to see me."

"What? You mean you've met this guy?"

"No, but when I finally do meet him, I want to be a fresh face. I don't want to be just another rat he's seen at every card."

Straker guessed she had a point. He stood in front of her, letting her essentially hide behind him. The line of ringrats opposite them actually recoiled when the shadow emerged. "Go home Goon!" one yelled and threw a cup. Another yelled: "Don't you hurt Dare!" And another, "If you hurt Slick Dare I'll kill you!" Straker's brow rose at their seeming conviction; fake or not, these people were getting into this no less enthusiastically than if it were an NFL playoff game. But Straker's brow arched even further when he got a look at…

*Goon,* he thought. *Holy motherfucking shit…*

Straker doubted that he'd ever seen a more physically awesome—

or dangerous—human being in his life. The six-seven was no lie, and neither was the 350. In spite of the barrel belly, this was all muscle. Legs like carven tree trunks flexed beneath black full-length tights. Pectorals popped, the size of tortoise shells, and his arms were probably larger and stronger than the average man's legs.

Melinda peered from behind Straker's neck. "He bench presses 600, and can squat half a ton. He cracks coconuts between his knees."

"I believe it," Straker muttered. But scariest of all, somehow, was the black and red mask laced to his face. Deadpan eyes glared out through the holes. Teeth glittered in the tiny mouth slit. He looked like something more than human, or something less. *I wouldn't take that guy on with a five-shot Remington full of 10-gauge,* Straker determined. This guy was a human meat-rack, a walking chassis of convoluted muscle mass and bone structure. Even his shadow seemed awesome; it trailed behind him like a wicked mascot.

Melinda came back around once Goon stepped into the ring. The ring floor visibly wobbled under his weight. Dare strutted like a cock-sure rooster, taunting Goon with drowned out braggadocio. Goon only opened and closed his ham-hock-sized fists and stared the champion down.

Dare spun around, raised his arms to the crowd, then began to remove the Liberace robe. Straker could smell the "work" a mile away. With Dare's back turned, Goon charged, lifted him up, and pulled a hard belly-to-back suplex. Dare howled at the impact. And for the next fifteen minutes, Goon and Dare went at it with mutual pile-drives, bodyslams, armbars, and attempted sleeper holds. Straker was amazed, next, when Goon—weight and girth notwithstanding—rose into the air and fired a drop-kick to Dare's pretty-boy face. Dare flipped over the rope, landing on his back.

"The finish's coming up," Melinda said. "Watch."

Straker watched, somehow fascinated in spite of the knowledge that this whole thing was a sham. Goon stood atop the ringpost and—

"Holy shit!" Straker exclaimed.

—landed square on Dare's chest. Straker, by now, didn't care how fake this was. Ten feet onto cement was ten feet onto cement, with Dare between the flying rock and the hard place.

**74**

Goon jerked away, roared at the fans behind the rail, then snatched up a metal folding chair.

"The, uh, the chairs are fake, right?" Straker hesitantly queried. "I mean, like, they're plastic, right?"

"No," Melinda said.

Just as Goon turned, though, Dare revived himself, to the approval of the crowd. He tore the chair from Goon's grasp, and then—

WHAP!

—smacked the seat of the chair right smack-dab against the top of Goon's skull. Goon teetered as Dare did a loud "Wooooo!" right to his face. In another second, though, Goon had dove under the ring, and when he came back up, he was wielding a two-by-four.

The crowd shrieked. Dare backed off. Then—

Goon ran after the Wonder Boy.

The two-by-four made several audible swipes past Dare's face. A final swipe, however, dangerously close, was caught by the 12-time heavyweight champion, wrested away, and then—

"Kill him!" several ringrats screamed.

Dare cut loose with another "Wooo!" and then—

"Bust his head!" Melinda screamed.

*Women,* Straker thought, *are so violent!*

Dare slammed the two-by-four in a vast arch and broke it with a *crack!* over Goon's head. Goon fell, twitched once, then didn't move. Dare whooped it up as the ring announcer declared him the winner.

Two guys in phony paramedic suits buzzed out, hoisted Goon onto a stretcher, and whisked him back to the locker room.

"Did you see?" Melinda asked. "Did you see how hard Dare hit him with that two-by-four?"

Straker shrugged, the energy worn off. "It was a piece of Styrofoam with woodgrain on it."

"Yeah?"

When Melinda bent over the rail, Straker could do nothing else in the entire fucking world except eyeball her derriere. *I need to beat off again,* he thought. *Bad.*

But a moment later, the reporter was handing him one broken half of the phony two-by-four.

Straker smiled but then—

*What the—*

Something in his gut plummeted. Yes, he'd seen how hard The Wonder Boy had broken that piece of Styrofoam over Goon's masked head. The only problem was...

*This isn't Styrofoam.*

Straker hefted the splintered wood in his hand.

*This is real,* he realized. *That fuckin' guy just broke a real two-by-four over Goon's head...*

✪ — ✪ — ✪

"Down near Cotter's Field," said one chain-smoking, beer-gutted Richard Kinion, a cracker, a rube, and, namely, the Chief of the Luntville Police Department. Cotter's was an acreage of some of the finest soybean-planting land in the whole state, and Old Man Cotter and his boys sold it all to the Japs via some confalutin' new trade agreement. Fine with the Chief, though, even though his own daddy'd had his leg blowed off in some big ass-whuppin', fucked-up battle called Truk, some fuckin' sam-amm-ur-eye drove his Mitsubishi plane smack-dab into the 40-mike-mike deck on daddy's carrier, and daddy were one'a the loaders. Ain't *no way* Chief Richard Kinion'd *ever* buy a car made by the same evil, slanty-eyed Shintu worshippin' fucks that about *wore our asses out* in the big WW Two. "You buy yerdumbself a Dodge Colt'n—let me tell ya—you're payin' the same friggin' compernee that made the friggin' plane that tore ass on Pearl Harbor, that's what'cher doin'," the Chief could not help but prattle on a bit...

But back to Cotter's Field... "Cotter's—ya know where it is, son?" the Chief asked.

PFC Micah Hays cut a down-home shuck-and-jive hillbilly grin. "Shore do, Chief. Shee-it, Cotter's? We used to call it Cotter's Fuck Hole we did, 'cos'a all the poontang we'se used ta bust out there. Yes, sir, all's through high school all we hadda do is pick us up some white-trash splittail, a six-pack of Dixie, and next thing we know, Chief, we'se're humping ourselfs some redneck box till Kingdom Come, and I'se do mean *come!*"

Chief Kinion smirked as though he did not approve of such scato-logical verbosity from a fellow officer, but it was actually because he, in his younger days, was not so rewarded by any similar availability of women. "Just cut the dirty talk, son, and let me give ya the lowdown. Just got me a call from Tritt Tuckton, you know, that booger-eatin' cracker from up past old Grandpappy Martin's, and he says ta me he's walkin' down the Route just pretty as you please, but as he come up on Cotter's Field—"

"Yes, sir!" PFC Hays could not help but intervene. "Cotter's Field, shee-it! I'se *laid* me some peter out there, Chief, had my dick in dirty box more times than old man Cotter had his ass in a tractor seat! The dirtier the better, ya now, and praise God fer cracker gals, yes sir! If ya cain't smell that dirty hole a country mile away, then what good is it, tell me that? Ripe, *stanky* pussy's the best pussy. Grows hair on yer balls, yes sir. Leaves kind've a sheen on yer dick, lets ya know ya been fuckin' like a man next time ya pull'r out to have a pee. That dirty cracker pussy stank waft up and like ta *smack* you in your kisser! Says in the Bible God gives good works ta men, and He shore do by blessin' us country boys with feisty, dirty, box-stanky cracker gals, huh, Chief?"

Chief Kinion's stomach did a hitch, and his brow furrowed at this rather inordinate observation. In addition, he rather doubted that the Lord on High had cracker gals in mind when He thought to bestow good works upon men. Not that the Chief could very well relate to the young PFC Hays either way as he had not had his bone in any pussy—stinky or otherwise—for quite a spell. Take his wife Carleen, for exam-ple: a slim purdy pixie when he married her some twenty years ago but like most slim purdy pixies she shore as shit stopped puttin' out about two days after she said "I do" on the altar of Grace Baptist Church. Turned to fat just as quick such that, now, Chief Kinion would often awake in the middle of the night and wonder why in tarnation there was a 1200-pound Berkshire hog snoring right next to him in bed, and fart-ing and belching and what have you.

He gritted away the image, and belched himself then. Those jumbo barbequed ham hocks he'd socked down into his breadbasket for lunch were mighty fine. $1.99 a plate down at Miss June's Diner, and he's had three plates. *Eerp.* A man could tell a good hamhock from bad, by the belch. "Anyway, Hays, like I was saying, we got this call from Tritt, says he sawed something awful up at Cotter's Field, said it were like a—"

"Yes, *sir!*" PFC Hays slapped his knee. "I 'member one time me'n Duke Caudill'n Harley Mack Reed was drinkin' down the Crossroads, an' in walks Sarah Sue Natter. About six months preggered she was, and we all knowed that anyways 'cos it already were all over town 'bout how she'd been fuckin' her pappy since she were about two. Anyways, she walks right up'n tells us she'll fuck us all she did, so we threw her horny tush'n big milk-filled titties in the back'a Duke's beat-ta-shit Chevy pickup, and drove straight ta Cotter's Field we did, an' Chief, we, I say we fucked that gal in the dirt fer *hours,* an' she's screamin' and comin' the whole time, and beggin' fer more at the top'a her lungs the likes'a which I thought shore they'd hear her clear over in Big Rock. 'Harder, harder!' she kept yellin' at us an'—shee-*it!*—we fucked that cracker's poon *hard,* Chief, so hard you could hear the milk shoshin' in them big hooters'a hers—big as a pair'a 'lopes like you'd find at Grimaldi's market fer half-a-buck apiece they was—an' I'se *swear* we each put four loads'a the petersnot in that box—*each* of us now, no lie—this fiesty white trash bitch done *drained* our balls, Chief, but even after takin' four squirts'a our nut up her hole—that's four squirts *each,* Chief—twelve total—she's *still* beggin' fer more, an' a'course we all knowed it probably weren't too cool gang-bangin' the funnelcakes'n wax beans outa gal while's she were preggered but, hail, Chief! she just kept askin' fer it so we thought it only gentlemanly ta oblige the lady's wishes. So's I'm on top'a her I is, humpin' away on her box a mile a minute, lookin' ta have me my fifth nut'a the night when—bam!—she up'n shriek ta wake all the dead in Beall Cemetery, an' then I hear a sound like dry branch'a birch crackin', so's I'se git offa her and look down an' I *swear's* I was lookin' at a pile'a roadkill comin' out her pussy. Yes, sir, we fucked that dog-horny cracker *so hard* she up'n had a mistercarriage right plumb smackdab in the middle'a Cotter's Field and all them soybean plants, she did! So's I'm lookin' in all that muck and I kin even see the little critter in there!"

"Fer Gawd's sake, Hays!" Chief Kinion fairly bellowed. A lurch in his gut and then a hard swallow. "This shit yer talkin's about to make me upchuck!"

"Ain't shit, Chief, s'true," Hays went on with his tale, "an' a'course afterward me'n Duke'n Harley Mack, we felt a might bad 'bout what happened—fuckin' her so hard she hadda mistercarriage—an' we told her so. But you know what she did, Chief, an' I'se *swear* this is true. She git herself up from that big mess, brush herself off all smilin' and then she say 'Thanks, boys! Didn't want that critter in me no ways—problee come out retart anyhow on account it were my daddy's juice that made it. See yawl later!' Then she up'n plumb walks away leavin' that critter'n that big roadkill-lookin' mess fer the possums ta eat."

Chief Kinion's face felt bloated and hot from the imagery, and those pieces of hamhock in his breadbasket began to boogie. "Gawd Almighty, son, that there's about the most disgusting thang I ever did hear," he croaked, wiping his brow off on a shirtsleeve.

"Shee-it, Chief," Hays rebutted, "that ain't nothin', 'cos, see, there was this other time when I'se picks up Kari Jane Wells hitchhikin' down the Old Governor's Bridge Road, 'an—ooo-ee!—she was lookin' a *might* fine she was! Cutoffs crawlin' up the crack'a her ass, and them big high titties on her stickin' out 'neath this yeller halter. Long blond hair down the middle'a her back and them long tan legs…shee-it, I'se gittin' wood just thinkin' 'bout her. Anyways, I picks her up an' first thing she does, she smiles at me'n says, 'Micah Hays, if yore a real man you'll drive us straight ta Cotter's Field 'cos I'se am a woman in some *dire* need!'" PFC Hays cut a grin. "Shee-it. I about come just by hearin' her say it so *a'course* I drive ta Cotter's, an' we ain't out there two minutes 'fore we'se both rollin' 'round in them soybeans like *buck* nekit and my cock's *rock*-hard'n ready ta tussle, yes sir! But just 'fore I'm gonna spread them long tan legs an' sink my pecker in her, she up'n say somethin' like 'Um, uh, I don't thinks ya wanna put it there, Micah,' an' I say, 'What'choo talkin' 'bout Kari Jane! A fella hafta be queer to not wanna put his bone in you!' so all she say after that it, 'Take a looky,' and she spread them legs, Chief, an' pointed ta her box, an' I 'bout blow chunks right there on Cotter's soybean plants, 'cos, see, Chief, Kari Jane's poon, it were—oh, lordy!—it were like—"

The Chief stolidly flicked a butt out the cruiser window. "Put a lid on it, Hays. I don't thank I want's ta hear no more—"

"—it were like…*infestered,* Chief! I take me a look at that pussy on her and it's *all* swollered up with pusserknots'n pimples'n vagereal warts'n these big red sores'n such. Shee-it, it were a cryin' shame, Chief—good-lookin' as she was but ya cain't fuck her on account she got herself a pussy fulla disease! It looked like a pile'a crushed raspberries her poon did! Like ta wanna slap her right upside the head fer ruinin' that box with all them infectsherins'n dieasers, an' I'm hard as a fuckin' *rock,* see, needin' ta squirt'a load in a big way but—shee-*it!*— I weren't stupid enough ta put my dick in *that* mess—"

"That's enough, Hays," the Chief ordered, more imagery spilling into his head, more tremors in his gut.

But Hays wouldn't hear of it. "Fella'd hafta be *crazy* to lay peter in that, no matters *how* dog horny he is, so I'se say, 'Well good gawddamn Kari Jane! What'choo you bring me all's the way out here ta Cotter's Field just ta show me a pussy I wouldn't fuck with a *dog's* dick?' But she just smile and git up on her hands'n knees, lookin' back over that purdy shoulder'a hers, an' she say 'Ain't got no dieasers in my ass, sweetie,' an' I'se kin tell ya, Chief, it were the finest ass I ever did see, an', no sir, it didn't have no sores'r pusserknots on it like her pussy did, so's I did what any red-blooded boy'd do. I spit on my pole an' popped're right in there, Chief. Weren't too tight, I must say, but I don't 'spect mine were the first crotch rocket ta go up her backside— but a nut's a nut, hail. So I pump that tail *hard,* Chief, holdin' her face down in the dirt while's I'se doin' it, and then I have me a *good* come, I did, popped my snot right up inta the middle'a her shit, yes sir! Ain't drained my balls like that in coon's age; I'se come so much, n'fact, almost felt like I was *peein'!*"

"Hays, in holy blazes would you shut the fuck up," Chief Kinion groaned at the wheel—

But PFC Hays, regrettably, would *not* shut the fuck up, because when he had a story to tell, by God, he'd tell it through to its conclusion. What good was a story, after all, without an ending? The young officer chortled in his shotgun seat, even gave his crotch an errant rub. "I'll tell ya, Chief, women, they can be downright dag dirty bitches when they wanna be. Act like little angels when they'se prancin' the street but when they'se git their clothes off, none of 'em ain't nothin' but a buncha fuck-pigs...and thank God for 'em. 'Cos see, Chief, after

I blew that big nut up her ass, I'se pull my bone out, and she turn an' push me back in them soybean plants an' say 'Don't'choo thank yer gonna run off just yet, Micah Hays, 'cos we ain't quite finished yet. See, I'se gonna suck you clean!' an' I'se look down at my dick, ain't enough time even passed fer me ta lose my stiffer, but I see—aw, lordy, Chief—my dick were just *caked* with her shit, see, and what's even worser is this—"

"Shut up, Hays! Just shut—"

"—is that her shit's got all this *corn* in it, ya know, but that don't bother her none, I'se swear, an' then she suck my dick just like she promised—got back a full stiffer an' even came again I did, put another load'a my snot right down her yap! But that ain't all that when down her yap, Chief, 'cos when she's finished I'se look at my dick again, it's clean as a *whistle,* yes sir, an' all that shit'n corn is *gone!* And then she look at me, Chief, and she smiles'n says 'Micah Hays! That there was the *best* corn on the cob I ever had!'"

Chief Kinion pulled over and before he could even bring the Luntville police cruiser to a full and proper stop, he threw up out the window in one large, pulsing basso-profundo gust after another. Up it all came, and then out in hot splatters: buttered home fries and sweet onions, a couple cups of java, and three full plates of barbequed hamhocks from Miss June's Diner for $1.99 a plate.

✪ — ✪ — ✪

Some time later, Kinion and Hays branched off through Cotter's Field. Problem was, that old rummie Tritt Tuckton didn't say where this ravine was exactly, and the Chief, especially after upchucking like a Navy bilge pump, wasn't too keen on spending the rest of his watch tramping his 260-pound caboose through this soybean field. But then—

"Hey, Chief, over here!" Hays called out some fifty yards off. "I'se found it, and..."

Kinion got on the hump, his size 13s crunching through the ankle-high rows. Looked like some kind of irrigation ditch before the wood-line. But Hays had just turned after his announcement, and his face had turned to blanched porridge.

"What the hail's wrong with you, boy?" Chief Kinion inquired, huffing up. "Look like you seen a ghost."

"Aw, shee-it. Tritt Tuckton weren't joshin' us, Chief. He said there were something awful in that there ditch, and he were right."

"What, what is it?" Kinion sniped. "I'm supposed to guess?"

Pale-faced, PFC Hays held up a feeble hand. "All's I can say, Chief, is it's a dag good thang you already blew chow. Wish I had, though, fer shore…"

And with that, the younger officer bent over, hands on knees, and began to loudly vomit.

*Jesus Chrast! What are we, the Puke Patrol?* Chief Kinion testily wondered. He didn't wonder long, however—he didn't have to. The stench was hitting him already, and then he ventured up and looked into the ravine…

# PART THREE

ack in the car, Straker still felt sick, remembering the distinctive sound of the two-by-four. "How did he do it? You're telling me that was part of the 'work'?"

"It was, Captain," Melinda asserted behind the wheel.

Straker exclaimed, "But that goddamn two-by-four was real! I held it in my hand! I guarantee you, this guy Goon? You don't have to worry about him anymore because he's dead!"

"He's not dead, Captain," she coolly replied. "He's not even hurt."

"I don't believe it. I don't care how big or tough a guy is, no one can take a chop to the head that hard without either dying or winding up in the emergency room with a fractured skull and subdural hematoma."

"That's just one aspect of Goon's uniqueness. There are...quite a few others," she said. "But I'm gonna help you get him. So help me God, I'm going to see Goon taken down and see to it that he spends the rest of his life in prison."

This was simply too much to calculate. Ringrats. Wrestlers. Works and cards and "grapplers." This wasn't Straker's world. But, evidently, it *was* part of hers.

"You're really into this stuff, aren't you?" he dared ask.

"So what if I am? My indoctrination into the world of ringrats and wrestlers has given me a closer look at the phenomenon. So, yes, Captain Straker. I guess I am into it a little."

Straker fudged. There was too much he couldn't reckon. "So where are we going now?"

She waved a finger like a teacher in class. "There are three ways a ringrat snags a grappler. One, you wait by the back exit door and hope somebody likes the way you look when they walk out to their cars. Two, you blow the security guard to get inside—"

Straker's cognizance snapped to attention. Just hearing her say the word—*blow*—roused his senses. "Have you done that? Have you *blown* security guards to get inside?"

"And, three," she didn't answer. "You go to the nearest bar and you wait. Most grapplers drink heavy. You wait there, see who shows up, and try to make your mark. An industrious ringrat can snag a grappler any night she wants."

"Yeah, yeah, but just answer my question. Have you blown security guards in order to gain access to the locker room?"

"What difference does it make to you?" she sniped back.

"Well, let's just say I'm curious."

"Sounds to me like you're jealous."

"Don't be ridic—"

"Yes," she interrupted. "I've blown security guards to gain access to the locker room. I've done a lot of things, Captain. I do whatever it takes for a story and, besides, I have needs to be taken care of too."

"I don't think any story calls for the kind of moral and sexual negligence that you're talking about, Ms. Pierce."

"That's not a surprising comment, Captain Straker. Coming from a guy who doesn't give a shit about how vigorously criminals are allowed to victimize the innocents of this world."

"That's a bit much, isn't it?" he shot back.

"No, it's not. Some cops are willing to go the extra mile, and—" She snapped her gaze right to his face. "—some cops aren't."

He wasn't going to argue. She was just like any other woman he'd ever known—she was nuts. It didn't matter that she was more beautiful than anyone he'd ever seen in his life. *She's nuts,* he thought. *She's out of control.*

"So, what? We're going to some bar now, in hopes to meet wrestlers?"

"Don't talk to me anymore," she said.

"Gimme a break."

"Just leave me alone. And I'm ashamed to say this, but…I was beginning to like you."

That perked him right up. "Oh, yeah?"

"But not anymore. You're just like all male cops. All you give a shit about is your fucking pension. Don't make waves, oh no. Don't risk engaging in alternative protocol in order to get the job done. Just slide along nice and safe."

"Alternative protocol, huh?" he objected. "You're forgetting one thing. Cops are bound to legalities. What you call alternative protocol a judge would call sexual malfeasance. I wonder what your editor thinks about spending the paper's money to shack up and party with wrestlers when you 'have needs to be taken care of'."

"Yeah?" She laughed sardonically as she pulled into a parking lot peppered with cars. "Then I guess I'll just have to tell your deputy chief, as well as everyone else at your headquarters, that you beat off three times in my motel room."

Straker's face turned red in a blink. His rage steamed along with his embarrassment. "You wouldn't dare—"

Melinda Pierce shrugged. "And that's a case in point. You won't go that extra mile. You won't take a chance to get the job done. You'd rather shirk away and beat off than take a crack at the real thing."

What did that mean? Straker's eyes bloomed; his entire *face* bloomed at the contemplation. Was she just being metaphorical, or did she mean that he actually stood a chance at—

"Wait a sec," he bid. "Let's talk about this."

But already she'd parked the car, got out, and slammed the door. Straker hustled after her. Up ahead a gaudy neon sign loomed over a roadhouse tavern: BIG JUD'S. Her high heels snapped across the gravel. By the time Straker had caught up, she'd already entered the bar.

Inside, he saw that she was right; this dump of a tavern was populated by many of the wrestlers he'd seen on tonight's card, only now they'd shed their tights and robes for street clothes. In addition, many of the same ringrats he'd seen loitering about the rail were here too, swooning over the grapplers, trying to edge their way closer. Two brunettes fawned over Dashing Dick Dude, feeling his biceps in awe. A hot redhead looked ga-ga-eyed at The Maniac, who chugged daiquiris one after another. And at a corner booth, Slick Dare sat with five rats, hamming it up and plying them with drinks.

Melinda stepped up to the bar, ordered a Coke. When Straker stepped up beside her, she grimaced and said, "You still here?"

"Listen, let's talk."

"I don't work with wimps," she retorted. "Go call a cab, go home. I'll do the job myself. Shit, I thought your people were going to assign me to a professional, not a candyass."

"I am not a candyass," Straker objected. "I have the highest conviction rate of anyone in the state police."

"Give yourself a medal. Pay phone's over there. Call a cab and get out of here. Need a quarter?"

*What a hardass! This girl's breaking my chops like there's no tomorrow!* "All right, listen—"

"You're still here?"

Straker grit his teeth. "I've been thinking about this—" and he had, hadn't he? And it was true; he was being the perfect hypocrite, disparaging her for what she referred to as "alternative protocols" when he'd done the self-same thing just this morning with Traci Wilcox, the chicken lady.

Laughter exploded from Dare's table. "I'm a licensed pilot!" he bragged. "Woo!" He drained a gin and tonic in one gulp. "I own six gyms in North Carolina! Woo!" He flexed his pecs. "I am stylin' and profilin'! I'm the biggest and the best! Woo!"

*What a dick,* Straker thought. *And she thinks he's hot?*

Over his other shoulder, though, he could see the Fabulous Ghoula and Terri Strong—bitter enemies an hour ago—trading jokes over drinks. Then he looked at Melinda again, the flawless feminine line rising from her heels to her neck, the perfect, tanned legs jutting from the denim skirt, the white-blond hair and the world-class bosom.

"I'll do it," he said.

She smirked through a sideglance. "You haven't got the nuts."

"Watch me."

Straker steeled himself, took a deep breath, and parted. He approached Ghoula's table and before he was even halfway there, the blob-like, rat-haired woman looked up and shot a gapped grin.

"Sweetcakes!" she exclaimed. "I knew you'd come lookin' for me!"

Straker sat down at the table, winked at her. "I've still got that package for you, Ms. Ghoula. What do you say we go back to your motel and open it together?"

✪ — ✪ — ✪

Melinda couldn't help but smile. *That poor sucker, he's in love with me.* She watched amused as Captain Straker snagged his mark and eventually left the bar with the Fabulous Ghoula on his arm. But Melinda had some snagging to do herself, and time was wasting. *Be industrious,* she thought. Dare was sitting over there with a veritable harem, but Melinda knew her own looks blew them all away. She finished her Coke, then traipsed over. The other rats at the table glared at her.

"Get out of here, bitch," one flat-chested girl remarked. "Can't you see this table's full?"

"Too bad your bra's not," Melinda replied.

"Buzz off, Blondie!" barked a brunette with way too much eyeliner.

"Is that mascara, or did somebody punch you in the eye?"

"Fuck you!"

Melinda ignored them. She leveled her gaze at Dare. "Hey. Wonder Boy. You gonna hang out in this dog pound all night, or are you gonna jump some real bones?"

Dare only stared at her, his gaze locked on her haltered breasts, her tight waist, her knock-out hips and Penthouse legs.

Melinda, without hesitation, smoothly removed the halter. "How'd you like to pin *these* to the fuckin' mat?" she said.

That was all it took. Dare dropped a c-note on the bar, and stood up. "I only have one thing to say about that, baby."

Melinda ran her hands up, cupped the melon-tight 38Ds. "Yeah, Wonder Boy? And what's that?"

Dare shot his cuffs, did a quick pec-flex, then hauled back and shouted, "Woooooo!"

# GOON

*Oh, for Christ's sake,* Melinda thought. *Hurry up and come!*

Alternative protocols or not, she was really getting sick of this. Right now, she lay naked and squashed under the 243-pound frame of The Wonder Boy Slick Dare, and he was humping as though she were nothing more animate than a watermelon with a hole in it. At least if the action was good, she might be able to get into it, but even the roughest of them—like Fantastic Freddie Faylor and Kevin the Druid—bored her to tears. The closest she'd gotten so far was a few weeks ago, when Brian Orndorf and Paul Blair had play-raped her on Orndorf's kangaroo-skin throw rug. They'd let her fight back a little, and she'd gotten to take some shots, but all it left her with in the end was an unfulfilled spark between her legs.

But after hauling the ashes of close to thirty of these well-muscled morons in the last month, she felt she deserved at least one orgasm for her trouble. *Men are all a bunch of pussies,* she dismissed. *Won't try anything knew 'cos it might bruise their macho egos.*

When they'd first gotten back to the HoJo room, Dare's roomie, Slapjack Culligan, was pouring drinks. "Hey, Cullie, look at the prize I found," Dare bragged, dragging off a black t-shirt bearing a silver stallion. Culligan, in a leather vest, chaps, and Texas shitkicker boots, gave a whistle. Melinda nodded a cordial hello, then winced when Dare climbed out of his jeans, sporting a limp penis drooping like a dead lizard, a *big* dead lizard. It was bigger limp than most men were hard. Then he downed a gin and tonic like a shot, poured another, and did it again. *Jesus,* Melinda thought. *Drink much?*

"Get outa them panties, hon. Show the boys what you got."

Melinda shrugged, did it, and flung the panties on the bed. Slick Dare gaped at her obvious lack of pubic hair, then Slapjack chuckled and commented in his hick Texas drawl, "Ain't you heard the rule, honey? No hair, no Dare."

"Well," Dare jumped in, "I usually dig a plot of hair that'd knock your Aunt Connie's socks off, but—*Woooo!*—this piece of fuck pie is so hot, the Wonder Boy can make an exception."

*Piece of fuck pie,* Melinda thought. *We'll see about that.* She assumed this Slapjack cracker would be part of the ride, but that was no big deal. Threesomes, foursomes, *room*somes—she didn't care so long as she got what she wanted. It would be nice, though, for some diversity tonight, and just as she'd thought it—*What the hell?*—she turned at the sound of bedsprings.

Slick Dare was jumping up and down on the bed, and he was—
*Oh for Christ's sake!*
—he was wearing Melinda's red panties.

A ludicrous sight if there ever was one: big, tan, muscled, and blond, here was Slick Dare the Wonder Boy, the adopted son of a rich midwest doctor, jumping up and down on HoJo mattress wearing women's underwear. The half-hard dick poked out above the waistband—like a sea slug or something—and Dare, with each trampoline-like jump shouted: "Wooo! Wooo! Wooo!"

Melinda could only stare in disbelief. This was not the kind of diversity she had in mind. "He gets a little silly after he drinks," Slapjack whispered. "Have fun." Then he left.

✸ — ✸ — ✸

And now, later...

Dare's penis fairly burrowed into her. Nine and a half inches; the asshole had actually put a ruler to it as proof. It was big, all right, but Melinda was an accommodating gal. He was fucking her nearly to sleep, the motel bedsprings squeaking annoyingly, his groin slapping. Every so often, his cock would slip out and she'd have to reach down and guide it back in. It felt like an oiled Italian sausage. A half hour later the scene hadn't changed. These assholes would drink all night, so it took them forever to come. Dare humped and humped and humped, steady as a piston in an engine cylinder and about as exciting as a bowl of unflavored yogurt.

Eventually her thoughts drifted to Captain Straker. *I hope he's having more fun than me...*

✸ — ✸ — ✸

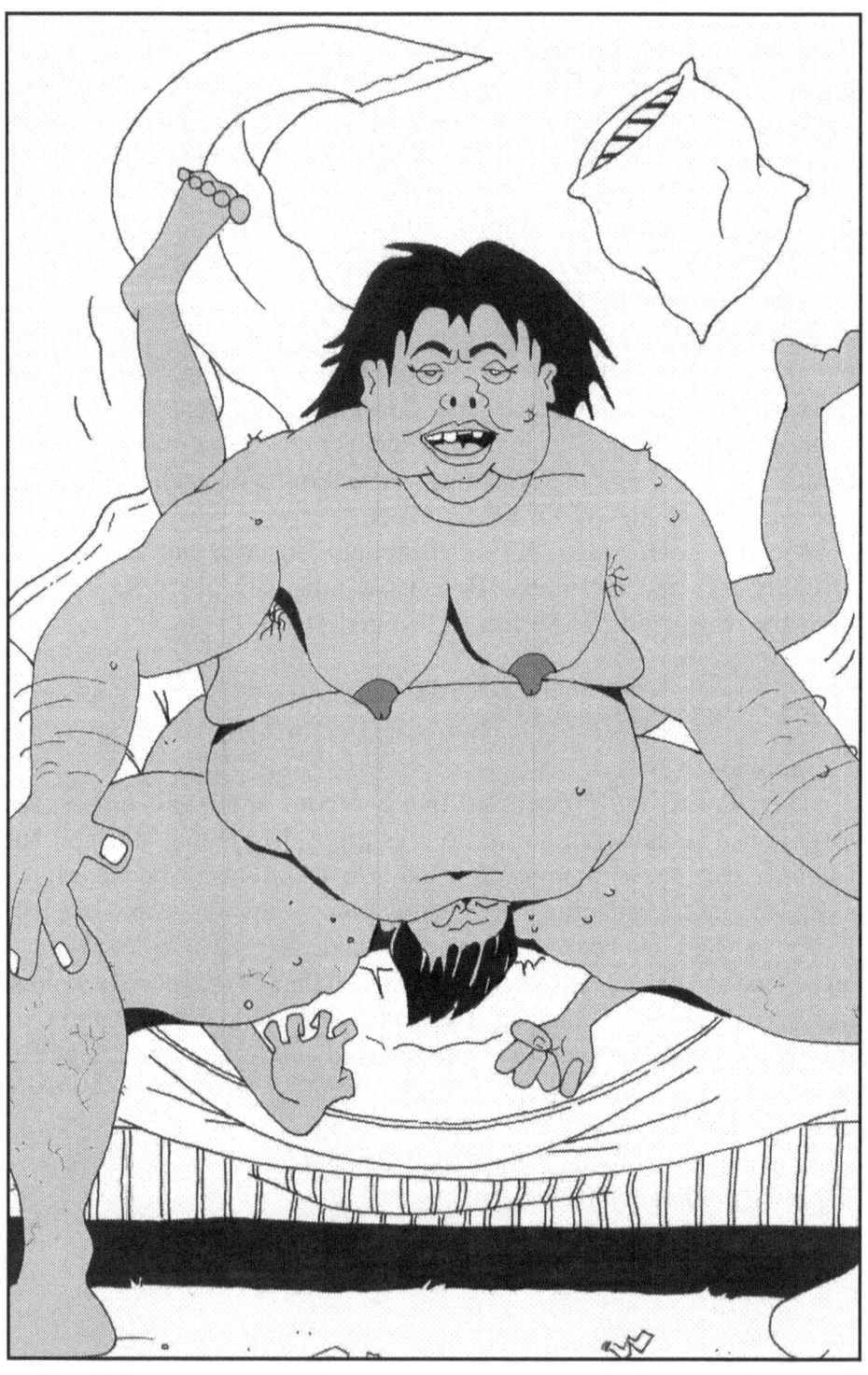

"That's it, sweetcakes! Tongue that great big honey-hole for Ghoula! Lick that clit like a lollipop!"

The physical act of the Fabulous Ghoula sitting on Straker's face made him feel as though his entire head were being engulfed by some huge, pallid sea slug. He lay stiff on the motel bed, paralyzed, his eyes shock-wide as the amorphous female grappler kept the nightmare pubis pressed snug to his face. Every so often, she'd lean forward in her ecstasy and block Straker's nostrils, whereupon he'd helplessly flop, squirm, and cringe until she got the message that he was close to smothering. Looking up from this vantage point showed him a mountain range of ascending white blubber, with two foot-long avalanches that were breasts. A few wire-like hairs sprouted from pores on nipples that looked like stepped-on persimmons. Worse than this vision, though, was the tactility of the entire scenario. Straker's tongue did its best to oblige her wishes, often losing its bearings in a vaginal opening that could only be described as a morass. It sat plopped on his face like the mouth of a great sucker fish, constricting once in a while, and drenching his chin, neck, even his upper chest with a nefarious sheen. Blubber settled on either cheek, a hot vice of pocked lard, and sometimes the weight of her inchoate buttocks threatened to crush his ribcage like a taco shell and separate his head from his shoulders.

*Please, God. Just let me die...*

The pancake breasts and ground-pork majora of the chicken lady seemed like as beautiful as a *Sports Illustrated* swimsuit model compared to this. A clitoris the size of an acorn hardened against his tongue, beyond which occasional careless delvings revealed clusters of fibrotic cysts.

"Yeah, sweetcakes! You are one hot tongue-fucker!"

Straker did not appreciate the compliment. He gasped in momentary relief, though, when she suddenly inclined herself off his face. At first he thought she was done, but then a deeper horror assailed him when he noticed that she was merely traversing her position. "Let's take a drive down Route 69!"

*Let's not,* Straker thought. Now her feedbag buttocks settled monstrously on his face, his nose pressed into a rank abyss. "Let me give ya some workin' room back there, huh?" she was kind enough to offer, and with both hands reached back and parted the gelatinous rump. *Let me die,* he thought again. But that would be the easy way out. The bottom of her vulva drooped now, a pair of rooster wattles, and the highest scope of his vision showed him the collided moons of her sagging, white Sasquatch caboose, highlighted by tiny red butt-pimples you could use to play connect-the-dots. But this was a vision of heaven when compared to that opened crevice of ass-crack. Straker imagined Bosch-like visions of hell, beaked demons shouldering from the puckered rictus to pull off strips of his living flesh and clip off extremities like carrot-ends. Yes, this woman's ass-crack was truly a vision of hell. Gilles de Rais would flee in horror. Even Satan himself would wince. That pitlike pink-brown starburst of an anus. Had Straker ever seen anything scarier in his life?

No.

Trace hair lined the groove, littered with dinkleberries. Her anus looked like an empty eye socket, complete with lashes, and it was no secret that she hadn't been very thorough about wiping after her most recent Number 2. Now Straker was pitted against a paramount effort to see how long he could hold his breath and perform cunnilingus at the same time.

"Aw, sweetcakes! How selfish of me!"

With this remark, she offered some attention herself, attention of the oral persuasion, settling forward like a white manatee and taking his entire scrotum into her mouth at once. She sucked his balls like a bag of gumdrops, yet his penis felt dead. Dead meat. The head of a turtle trying to retract back into its shell. Soon he would be history's first man to sport internal genitalia.

Eventually, she liberated his scrotum with a wet smacking noise. "How's that for a ball-suck, honey? Hmmm?" Then she took the dwindling strip of flesh that was his cock wholly into her mouth.

Straker squeezed his eyes shut. Concentrated. But—

Nothing. Dead.

"Come on, sweetcakes. Get this love-stick hard for your baby."

Straker could fabricate no manner of imagery sufficient to stiffen his "love-stick." Her mouth sucked it out like a piece of taffy—a very *small* piece of taffy—and soon the Captain of the State Police Violent Crimes Unit realized his full dilemma. If he did not rise to the occasion,

she'd more than likely be offended and, hence, not inclined to be forth-
coming with what she knew about Goon or his manager. This, after all,
was the real reason he was here. And what would Melinda say if he
failed so totally?

But that thought—just that mere name: Melinda—rolled through
his mind like fine brandy in a snifter.

*I'm going to do this,* he resolved. *I'm going to go the extra mile and
prove to her that I'm not a candyass!*

And resolve he did. He bravely redirected his cunniligual efforts,
riding like the Six Hundred into the Valley of Death.

"Ooo, sweetcakes, that's good," she abruptly praised. "Thought I
was losin' ya there for a minute, but—hot damn—you eat box lunch
with the best!"

Box lunch, indeed. He was going to make this a Thanksgiving din-
ner. He was going to make this mammoth of a woman have an orgasm
if it killed him. And as for his own responses…

*Melinda,* he thought.

Now that was the ticket. *Just think about her,* he commanded himself. *Think about Melinda…*

*Kissing Melinda…*

*Touching Melinda…*

*Putting your arms around Melinda…*

*Making love to Melinda…all…night…long…*

Straker's cock came alive in Ghoula's garbage-sump mouth.
"Mmmmm," she responded. "Mmmmmmmmmm!" Soon she was fel-
lating the whole thing, from hilt to glans, all six-and-half mighty, strap-
ping, woman-killer inches. Simultaneously, the Captain lapped and
lapped and lapped, until the weight above him began to flex, squirming
in unbridled delight. *Melinda, Melinda, Melinda,* he thought over and
over and over. Fibrotic cysts be damned! Yeast and stink and butt-pimples—kablooey! Straker's tongue became the Warrior of the
Apocalypse, fearless now on this treacherous hunting ground. It bravely licked and sucked and laved, striding ever onward to victory. Even
the dinkleberries caused not a flinch. Not even the poop smudges nor
hair-fringed rectum itself. Like a trooper, Straker conquered all, and
soon she was coming like an 18-wheeled Peterbilt with no brakes. "Aw,

sweetcakes!" she paused long enough to exclaim amid squeals and moans and even shrieks. "Aw, aw! Awwww!" She gasped, then screamed. "YES! YES!" she wailed in brass-horn tenor...

And came right in his face.

Her bulbous ass-carriage flexed off a few more spasms, then settled down along with her moans. With her orgasm came a veritable flood of vaginal fluids. *Pee in my face why don't ya?* Straker thought, but even with the flood he was not dissuaded.

Next, though, she very adroitly returned to her ministrations. The nightstick of his passion was tightly swallowed whole, then catered to in expert fashion. But as his thoughts flittered on, it was not the Fabulous Ghoula so nimbly sucking his dick.

It was Melinda...

And with that thought...

Straker strained, then popped enough semen into her yap to fill a shot glass. Drained as he may have been via today's multitudinous releases, Straker came long and hard right down the Fabulous Ghoula's throat. *I hope she likes egg-drop soup,* he thought and just kept coming. One spurt after the next, right down the hatch.

"Mmm, Christ," she said, smacking her lips when the jizz show was done. "You shoot a big nut, sweetcakes."

"Yeah," Straker replied.

She turned around, then lay beside him in bed. "Well, now I guess it's time—"

Straker assembled all of his potential play-acting talent, and... cuddled up right next to her. That's what women wanted, wasn't it? To be shown affection after the moment of crisis? He snuggled close, then even held her hand.

Her face screwed up. "What the hell are you doing?"

The query caught him off guard. "Well, I—I-I'm trying to be, you know... Affectionate."

"Oh, you're a hoot!" she replied and laughed like someone on Hee-Haw.

Straker blinked in confusion. He was halfway there now, but he still had the second half of his duties. He had to hit her up with questions about Goon and his manager.

"That was really a great time," he feigned. "Now I thought we'd just snuggle up."

She belted out another piglike guffaw. "Hate to tell you this, sweet-cakes, but the only thing you're gonna snuggle up with tonight is the parking lot."

Straker blinked again. He didn't get it. "What, uh, what do you mean?"

"What I mean is this. It's time for you to get the fuck out."

"You're…you're kidding me?"

"You got five seconds to haul on your duds and be outa here, pal. I've gotta drive to Lexington in the morning, and that's a three-hour haul, and I gotta be ready to wrestle an 8 p.m. card."

Straker stood up, naked, uncomprehending. "I see, well… If you don't mind, I'd like to ask you a few quick questions before I leave. See, I need to—"

The bed creaked. And it was a terrifying thing to behold as this monstrous woman got up. Hair frizzed out, gaps where teeth should be, and a physical frame comprised of layers, stacked like flapjacks, on two legs.

"This is my hand," she said, raising her big, meaty paw. "And this is my hand in your hair."

"OW!" Straker yelled as she grabbed him by the hair and gave a good hard twist.

"And this…is a door."

She opened it, giving his scalp a final torque, then shoved Straker into the parking lot.

Straker staggered up to stand outraged, humiliated, and buck naked. He cupped his genitals as his clothes flew out the door.

"Wait! I need to know about—"

The door slammed, loud as a gunshot.

Unbelievable. *All that work,* he thought, *for nothing.* And work was right. It was no picnic having that big pimply kiester in his face. He clumsily pulled his clothes on in the quiet parking lot, then shuffled off.

*Well… At least I tried,* he reasoned. He'd definitely gone the "extra mile" for the sake of the investigation, so Melinda certainly couldn't fault him for that. But the mere thought of her name, now, made him edgy. Extra mile or not, she'd probably give him a boatload of shit for striking out. And there was something else too, wasn't there?

*Melinda...*

Though he'd never admit it to her, he could admit it to himself. *Right now she's fucking Slick Dare. She's been changing this guy's oil for hours.*

Straker *was* jealous. He couldn't help it. And the imagery made him seethe: Dare's big mitts all over her flawless body, his cock in her. *That pompous, bleach-blond motherfucker's probably come in her five times by now.*

❋ — ❋ — ❋

"Shit," Dare muttered. "Can't come."

Melinda sighed, wincing, as Slick Dare rolled his tanned, sweat-sheened body off her. The rolling-pin-sized penis drew out of her with an audible click. Then he sat up on the bed and swigged a watery gin and tonic.

The massive shoulders shrugged. "Sorry, baby. Just one of those things, you know. Must'a drank too much tonight, can't get the gun off."

Melinda leaned up, quelled her outrage. *That asshole humped me for over an hour...* Even *her* pussy was sore.

Dare looked at his phony Rolex. "So look, baby. I can't get a nut tonight, so why don't you take off, huh?"

Astonishing. Men. What selfish, arrogant cads. *This is it? The dead-dick piece of shit can't come, so now he's kicking me out?* She did her playacting best to comfort him, rubbing his shoulders, a coo in her voice.

"Oh, don't worry, we can try again later."

"No can do, baby. Gotta get some sleep. I have to drive to Lexington in the morning. That's a three-hour haul, and I gotta be ready to wrestle an 8 p.m. card. I don't want to be rude but—let me put it this way: Get the fuck out."

Now Melinda's outrage came unquelled. She couldn't believe this was happening. She got up in a tizzy, put on her panties, her denim skirt, then stopped and glared at him.

"You got dirt in your ears, babe?" Dare asked. "I need you to beat feet."

Melinda snapped. "Beat feet? How about I beat your ass!"

"Come on, don't get bitchy now. You ringrats are gonna have to learn that you can't have it your way all the time." He swigged more of his drink, resonating his arrogance. "Let me tell you something— women stand in line for me. They get in fights over me. I did you a big favor just by letting you touch me. But the party's over now, so you gotta shag your ass out of here."

That was it. She'd had it. She was mad. "Well let me do *you* a big favor, Slick," she offered, then sauntered over.

SMACK!

She laid her palm across his face so hard his drink flew out of his hand and he fell off the bed.

"How do you like that, dickhead?"

Dare shook the shock out of his head, squinting up at her in disbelief. "Are you crazy? I'm the most successful professional wrestler of all time. You don't just slap someone like me. You're just a stringbean little ringrat. I could kick your ass in my sleep."

SMACK!

The second blow was harder. Dare stumbled, dizzy, as he rose from the floor. "You're going to the hospital now, bitch."

Melinda knew she shouldn't be doing this, she could blow her cover. But even she had her limitations for abuse. As Dare rose, she did a quick spin, then sunk a perfectly executed karate kick into his belly. Dare bent over, groaning like a just-gelded walrus. And when he looked up—

THWACK!

—she drove an equally perfect palm-heel right into his face. His nose broke with a crunch. Dare mewled and went down again.

"You wanna fuck with me, Wonder Boy? Come on. I'm waiting."

This was just too much fun. Dare teetered up again, his nose leaking blood, his eyes crossed. He launched a misguided fist, which Melinda ducked effortlessly. She spun again and had him in an armbar—a *real* armbar—then hurled him into the wall. He came at her again only to receive yet another karate kick, this one to the right cheek—THWACK!—then another to the left—THWACK!—which sent a tooth flying across the room. Lastly, and she figured appropriately too, she jumped, turned, and twisted in mid-air, and drop-kicked the invincible Wonder Boy square in the chest. Dare sailed across the room, cleared the dresser, and crashed to the floor.

Melinda paused to fix her hair in the mirror. Dare sidled over, moaning.

"Want more, Wonder Boy?"

"No," Slick Dare groaned, his mouth gushing blood.

She knelt down in front of him, grabbed his white-blond hair and twisted. "I'm tired of fucking around with you goddamn wrestlers. I want information, and you're gonna give it to me."

His eyes crossed as he peered at her. He spat out another tooth. "Information. What the hell... You're a ringrat."

"No I'm not, hammerhead. All you need to know is that I'm going to ask questions, and you're going to answer them. Then I'm going to leave and you're not going to say a word about it, right?"

Dare very unwisely paused, so she pressed her thumb into the middle of his broken nose. Dare howled.

"This is crazy, I'll have you arrested!" he'd bloodily objected.

"No, asshole, you want crazy, this is crazy," she corrected him, then quickly grabbed his hand and—crack!—broke his pinkie. Dare barked in pain. "And this?" she said. "This you might want to call *real* crazy," and with that she wrapped her long sleek legs around his neck and squeezed on a head-scissors.

A *real* head-scissors.

She lay back laughing as he flipped and flopped, her thighs pressuring down against his trachea. "I want to know about Goon, so start talking."

Dare palms slapped the carpet until she took the scissors off. When he could move, he desperately slid his butt into the corner of the room. "Please, no more..."

"Tell me about Goon."

His face screwed up in utter incomprehension. "Goon? He's just a heel. I don't know nothing about him, nobody does."

"You can do better than that," Melinda encouraged him, then hauled him belly-down onto the floor, straddled his back, and treated him to a chin-lock—a *real* chin lock.

He bucked under her, growling in pain. This was supposed to be business, not pleasure; nevertheless, Melinda's vagina throbbed like a pent-up cock, seeping through her devil-red panties. The violence just...turned her on so much. She couldn't help it. Her nipples distended like sparkplug ends, and her entire body seemed to swell in prickly heat. *Don't kill the asshole,* she had to remind herself. When she climbed off, Dare went slack. She nudged his head with her foot. "I'm waiting, Slickie. Tell me about Goon, or I'll wear your ass out."

"Goon," he mumbled, bloodying the carpet. "What the hell do you want to know about him for?"

"Don't piss me off unless you want a sleeper hold—a *real* sleeper hold."

He flopped over, his face like a busted cherry pie. "I— Jesus. Goon? Shit, nobody knows much about him. He's a flake. Nobody's ever even seen him without his mask on. I—I don't know anything about him..."

Melinda shrugged, her bare breasts surging. "I need to see him, where does he stay? Quick or it's Sleeper time."

"No!" Dare pleaded, red spittle flying. "Goon, Goon, let me think— Shit! What do you want to know?"

"I want to know where he and Felander stay."

"A-a mobile home! He stays in a mobile home! His manager drives him to the arenas."

"Yeah, Felander, and the Winnebago. I know that, Slickie. But where?"

Dare picked his terrified brain for answers. He looked a sight now: his white-blond hair sticking up in spikes, his bald-spot showing. And that big deflated dick laying limp in his groin like a rubber full of pudding.

Then he began to cry.

He began to blubber like a baby in this total defeat. The 12-time heavyweight champ had met his match. "Please don't hurt me anymore!" he blubbered. "Please don't! I got no idea—"

Melinda pinched his cheeks together. "When you first came to

DSWC, Felander was your manager. Shortly thereafter, he picked up Goon too."

"Yeah, yeah, but Felander dropped me a few weeks later," Dare struggled to explain. "He dropped Ghoula and Rod Stimmons and all of his heels. He just wanted to concentrate on Goon, I guess. It didn't make sense."

"Some things don't. But for the short time Felander was carrying you and Goon, what did they do? Where did they go between cards?"

Dare was sobbing openly now, a 243-pound bronze baby. If he was wearing diaper, he'd have shit in them. "Honest to God—I don't know!"

"I guess we'll skip the sleeper and get right into the figure-four, huh?"

"Noooooo!" Dare sobbed.

"Maybe if I broke your legs, you'd want to talk a little more." Melinda got up. This was such a charge: seeing the Wonder Boy cry and beg and plead. Just the thought of punching him up or cracking those sturdy shins like broomsticks made her so wet she was dripping in her panties.

"I think Goon's in trouble with the law," she explained. "That's why Felander keeps him out of the circuit motels and drives him to the cards in the mobile home. He's hiding Goon. But there's an oddity about Goon that I've discovered. At least once a week, he has to...go someplace. There's something he needs that has to be kept hidden, and Felander has to take him to this place on a regular basis."

Dare wept into his hands. "I don't know what you're talking about. What place?"

"I don't know, it's just some inconspicuous location. When you were still with Felander just after he picked up Goon, did you stay in the mobile home too?"

"Fuck no," Dare responded. "I gotta quarter-million-house in Charlotte. I stay in the motels during the cards, and I drive my red Corvette to the arenas. I'm successful. I'm a licensed pilot. I own a string of gyms. I don't need to shack up in some goddamn Winnebago to save money."

"So you're telling me you've never been in Felander's mobile home."

"No, I—" Dare's sobs hitched down a moment. "Well, there was one time—"

"Good boy. Now we're cooking." Melinda smiled down on him. "So you've been in the Winnebago. Did you go in the back, where Goon stays?"

"No, no, I rode up front with Felander. My car broke down at the Waynesville Coliseum, so Felander agreed to drive me to the next town, said I could sleep in the front seat. Anyway, I got shitfaced after the match like I always do, and I passed out while Felander was driving. It was real late, and we had to be in Roanoke the next day."

Melinda placed her foot on Dare's limp dick and scrotum, threatened to pop his balls like eggs. "Keep going."

"And-and we stopped somewhere, in the middle of the night."

"Um-hmm. Good. Now…where did you stop?"

More blubbering now. "I don't know. I was passed out. All I remember is waking up in the front seat. The Winnebago was parked, and Felander wasn't there."

"Where. Did you. Stop?"

"I don't know! I can't remember, I swear to God!"

Melinda slumped. "You can't remember? Well then I guess we'll just have to find a way to improve your memory."

"NO!" Dare screamed.

Melinda couldn't resist. Her feminine muscles flexed as she stepped over him and grabbed his ankles. "NO! NO! NO!" Dare bellowed on. Then she deftly applied the submission hold that Dare himself had made infamous: the figure-four leglock. She locked her legs up in his, then fell over onto her side, pulling up on Dare's crossed ankles as he howled in mindless pain.

"Remember anything yet?" she asked.

"Aw Jesus Christ please stop!"

"I'll break 'em, Slickie. I'll snap 'em like popcicle sticks. Don't believe me?"

She hauled up harder on his locked ankles, pressuring his shins very close to the point of fracture.

"Pluh-pluh-please don't break my legs!"

Melinda's sex felt like a hotpot full of steamy stew. When she flexed her legs to keep on the pressure, she nearly came. "If I break your legs, you'll probably never be able to wrestle again, Slickie. Then you'd have to get a real life. We can't have that now, can we?"

Again she hefted up, and again, Dare wailed, pounding his palms into the floor.

"Where was this place?"

"Wait! Wait! It was a—"

Melinda let up. "It was a what?"

"Ug-guh-guh…"

"Ug-guh-guh what?"

"A garage!" Dare finally wailed.

*A garage?* That would make sense. A garage would be isolated enough. She let up off his ankles some more. "You mean a garage on someone's house? Felander's house? Where does Felander live?"

"Aw, shit, I don't know, but, no, it wasn't that kind of a garage. It was— It was—"

"Don't jerk me around, Slick." She gave another twist—Dare barked.

"A storage garage! Now I remember! It was one of those places where you rent storage space! A bunch of garages!"

This too made sense, much more than a garage at someone's house. A house was easier to trace…

"Keep talking."

"I woke up in the passenger seat," Dare yammered. "It was real late. Felander wasn't in the Winnebago. I looked out the windshield and saw that we were parked in front of a long row of these storage garage things. The bay right in front was open, and could see a light on. A couple minutes later Goon walks out, gets in the back and that's it. Then Felander comes out too, closes the garage door and puts a padlock on it. Then he gets back in a drives away. I ask him where we're at, and he mumbles something about having to stop at this storage place to check some contracts or some shit."

"And what happened then?"

"I went back to sleep. The next morning I wake up and we're in Roanoke. Felander drops me off at the motor lodge, I call Triple-A, and get my car fixed, and that's that, no big deal. Couple days later Felander drops me. I tell him he's out of his mind if he thinks he's gonna make more money off Goon than me, but he doesn't care, and neither did I really. Couple times since then I've wrestled Goon. The work is always the same: he kicks the shit out of me, tries to attack me with a chair or a bat, then I come back and take him out." Only now was Dare simmering down, the waterworks shut off, his blood drying. "So that's the scoop on Goon. That's all I know. He's a great heel, he can take punishment like no one I've ever seen. The big promotions have offered him high-six-figure contracts a bunch of times, but he always turns them down. Shit, wrestling's my life, I'd do anything to be back in the bigtime. Only reason I'm here is because DSWC is the only conference that'll take me. But this fucker Goon's turning down big money with WWF and WCW. It's almost like the guy wants to stay smalltime."

"He does, Slickie, he *wants* to stay here," Melinda informed him. She unwrapped her legs, released the lock, thinking. "It's the safest way for him to go on. The big promotions wrestle all over the country, a different big city every night. But Goon knows he has to stay low, he can't risk the kind of exposure he'd get in WWF or WCW."

Dare blinked, shaking out of his pain. "Why?"

"Shut up," she griped and shoved him away. "You're not off the hook yet, grandpa. There's still one more question you gotta answer, and I don't have any more time to play games." Melinda got up, unzipped her purse, and pulled out a—

"Holy shit," Dare muttered.

—revolver and rubber glove. She slipped the glove on, cocked the revolver and got down on one knee, and put the gun to Slick Dare's mussed head.

"What the hell kind of ringrat are you?" his voice grated.

"The kind that doesn't fuck around." More power, more sweet violence humming through her blood. Holding the gun to Dare's head made her breasts ache, the swampy, damp excitement rising like high tide. But she mustn't get carried away. "I want to know—exactly—where this storage garage is."

Dare knew she wasn't kidding. His eyes shut, he chewed his lower lip as he strained to remember.

"Come on, Slickie. The clock's running down, and in a couple more seconds that bell's gonna ring."

"Route 29," he finally blurted. "That's it, I'm sure. I mean, I don't know exactly where, but I remember we were on 29 all night. It shouldn't be hard to find it, just look in the phone book for any storage garages off 29 between Waynesville and Roanoke. If I knew exactly where it was, I swear to God I'd tell you."

She looked at him, then uncocked the revolver. "Yeah, I guess you would." Setting down the gun she pulled a small bottle of lotion from her purse, slopping it liberally on the glove as she flexed her fingers and made a fist. "There's just one more thing, champ, you're going to get a little reward. Bend over and spread 'em, cause now as you like to say we're going to go to school… And if you tell anyone about any of this, not only will I track you down and kill you, but I'll wait for a few months while your career goes in the toilet. After all, how will the articles in the wrestling sheets read, '12-Time World Champ Beaten Up and Fist-fucked by Ringrat?' That'll really help with endorsements, won't it?"

"I believe you," Dare sobbed as he bent to comply.

❂ — ✪ — ❂

Straker flicked his butt when he heard her high heels ticking across the silent parking lot. "Where have you been?"

Preoccupied, she dug the judo stick key ring out of her purse. "You know where I've been; I was getting some answers from Dare." She unlocked the car very casually, got in, unlocked his side.

"For three hours?" he objected when he slid in next to her.

"Some things take time." She started the car, pulled away. "How'd it go with you and Ghoula?"

Straker simpered. "I didn't find out anything on Goon or Felander. When we were…done, she threw me out. I've never felt so humiliated in my life."

Melinda chuckled half-heartedly at the wheel. "She took your business, then threw you out?"

"Yeah."

"It's no big deal."

Straker glared in the dashlight. Her nonchalance infuriated him. He at least expected her to be mad for failing in his objective. "I just did sixty-nine with Jabba the Hut, and all you can say is it's no big deal?"

"It happens sometimes. You work someone hard, then they don't talk. But at least you tried. You went in there and gave it your best shot—"

*Boy does she know how to make a pun,* Straker thought.

"—and I'm proud of you for going the extra mile."

Well, at least that was some consolation. The sideglance nagged at him, however. The way she looked in the soft glow of the dashboard, the way her thighs splayed on the seat, the nipples jutting through the halter. It was that quick, his desire a hair trigger. Never mind that he'd already had half a dozen orgasms already today. *I need to beat off again. Bad.* Her breasts jiggled minutely over a pothole; her sleek hands gripped the wheel, and all he could envision was those same hands on him. What would it feel like? The sensation of being touched by her? *I'd come in my pants,* he knew. *Just like that. One touch and my Fruit of the Looms'd be full of my cock-snot, my joy juice, my wax,* he remembered Jan Beck's ungainly reference. *Come City...*

"Why are you always staring at me?" she asked.

"I'm not staring," he lied. Thank God it was dark—she couldn't see him blush.

"You're blushing."

"No I'm not!" he fired back. His mind raced. He could see the creamy white thighs, the denim skirt cut so high her crotch was nearly exposed. "I couldn't help but notice. What happened to your stockings?"

Another nonchalant chuckle. "I left them there."

This burned him. "Oh, so the Wonder Boy was so good you felt the need to leave him some trophies?"

"You don't know the half of it. But none of that matters." She glanced at him once. "That over-the-hill son of a bitch told me everything, Captain Straker." Then, quite uncharacteristically, she patted his thigh.

Straker nearly turned his shorts into Come City.

"This case will probably be over by tomorrow," she said.

# GOON

They stopped at a motor lodge along Route 29. "Look," she'd explained, "I'm too tired to drive you back to your HQ tonight. I'll get us a couple of rooms here on my expense account."

"Just get one room," Straker hastened. "We shouldn't squander money."

"I'll get us two rooms, Captain."

"I'll sleep on the couch."

"Two rooms. Two, as in separate." But when she came back from the night desk, she was frowning. "Looks like you got your wish, Captain. There was only one room left."

"Aw, that's too bad," he replied, his heart racing now. But what did he expect? He knew he wasn't going to put the make on her. *Maybe it's just...proximity,* he guessed. *Just being around her...*

"The Mayflower this ain't," he commented when they entered the motel room. "But— What a great couch!"

She didn't seem to hear him. Instead she hurried to the nightstand and opened the phone book. Straker lounged back on the couch, flicked on the TV with the remote, all the while eyeing her as she prowled the listings. She kicked off her high heels, curling her toes unconsciously in the carpet. Straker wished *he* could be the carpet.

"What are you looking up?"

She chewed on a pencil end, running a glossy nailed finger through the phone listings. "Midpoint," she said more to herself. "Waynesville and Roanoke..."

"What?"

"What towns are roughly midpoint between Waynesville and Roanoke along Route 29, Captain?"

"I don't know. Tylersville, maybe. Big Stone Gap."

"Yes! Here it is!"

Straker's brow crumpled. "Are you going to tell me what's going on?"

"Something Dare told me," she muttered and stood up. She closed the phone book. "Goon and Felander have a storage garage in Big Stone Gap. All the evidence you'll need should be there."

This information cruxed him. *Storage garage? Evidence?* But before he could ask, he winced when she bent over and poured herself a glass of water. The red panties peeked at him, satcheling the extrusion of her vulva like a neat little parcel.

"I think I know where they are, you can take it from here, Captain."

"Bullshit," Strkaer said. "What about your story? Don't you want to be there when we take him down?"

"That's not the way I am, Captain. I don't regard a grievous murder investigation as a way to accrue brownie points. I've got all the material I need now except for the follow up to the actual arrest, and I can get that from your report." She smirked out of place, then grimaced at the glass of water. "This water's terrible."

"They probably pump it in straight from the nearest creek," Straker posited. "But don't change the subject. We're in this together. When I bust Goon, I'd like you to be there."

"I'm too tired to argue." She pulled out some bills from her tiny purse. "Do me a big favor, will you? Go to that all-night Qwik-Stop across the road and get me a Coke."

"Not until you promise me that you'll come along for the finish."

"All right!" she flared, and thrust the bills at him. "Just get me a Coke, and get yourself something."

"Thanks, Mom. Can I buy some models too?"

She smirked again, bone-weary. "Don't forget the key. I'm taking a shower."

Just that word—shower—filled Straker's penis with blood. Because the word brought an image: Melinda in the stall, naked, all fresh skin, big tits and long legs, shining in the cascade.

Straker grabbed her judo stick with the keys on it and sulked out, checked to make sure the door locked behind him. He crossed the dead highway, the motel's sign throwing his long shadow before him. Each step he took toward the Qwik-Stop, though, brought a more pristine image of her. Was it her complete inaccessibility that taunted him so? No, just her beauty. Just her sheer, raving, unadulterated beauty...

At the Qwik-Stop he was reminded that this state had no liquor curfew. *I could really use a drink,* he decided. *After doing the box lunch with Ghoula? I could use several.* He picked up a six-pack of Bud and a 2-liter Coke, then paused. He knew the rube at the register was gaping at his ludicrously tight jeans and wrestling tee, but he didn't care. *Maybe if I spiked her Coke up a little,* he considered. *Maybe that would loosen her up. Hmmm...* He picked a half-pint of Everclear 190-proof grain alcohol off the rack, paid the eyeballing rube, and left.

The shower was still running when he got back. *Boy am I a shit,* he thought, and quickly clunked ice cubes in a glass, splashed in two fingers of Everclear, then filled the rest with Coke. A test sip proved that the grain had no taste at all. Then he plopped down on the couch with a beer, switching TV channels with the remote.

On the floor her small travel bag sat opened. SKIN SMOOTH read a box on top. He'd seen commercials for the same product, a depilatory—hair remover. Beneath that was a contact lens case, and beneath that lay tubes of vaginal lubricants, but he noted nothing in the way of birth control. He was tempted to actually root around in the case but figured it would be just his luck to get caught.

*Mind your own business,* he ordered himself, then went back to the TV remote. Toward the end of the dial...

*Give me a break!* Wrestling blared on the screen: Slick Dare landing a belly-to-belly suplex on a silly, face-painted Venom, who reportedly made 1.5 million a year. Dare mussed Venom's pretty boy blond hair, then mussed his face paint. "Kick his ass!" he shouted at Venom.

The shower squealed off. The bathroom turned Melinda's voice into a sharp echo. "What did you say?"

"Wrestling's on. Can you believe it? Four in the morning and they got this shit on the tube. What kind of a moron would watch wrestling at this hour?"

"Who's watching it now?" she came back.

*Funny.* "I'd just love to see somebody clean Dare's clock." He couldn't get rid of it—the absurdity. Right now there was a man on television who'd had sex with the woman in the shower only hours before. Jealous? Yes. Straker was insanely jealous. *I should be the one having sex with her,* came the cruel thought. *Not this asinine bleach-blond muscle rack.*

"Can I ask you a personal question?" he dared.

"No."

"I mean, you were with Dare for three hours. Did you—"

A wearied sigh echoed from the bathroom. "No, I didn't come, if that's what you're dying to know. I never do with wrestlers."

Straker's brow propped right up. "But you're the one who said these guys were hot."

"Oh, they're attractive, sure. Lots of muscles."

Straker felt his bicep, then slumped in despair. It felt like he didn't even have one.

Just then she emerged from the bathroom, a long towel cocooned her from breasts to thighs. She must not have washed her perfect white-blond hair though, for it hung shiny and dry to her shoulders. In fantasy, he saw himself unwrapping her like a package of immaculate flesh, then burying himself in her, being cocooned himself by her arms and legs.

*I need to beat off again. Bad.*

"Thanks," she said and sipped her jimmied Coke. "God, that's good."

*Better than you think,* he thought. She wandered over, stood next to him and looked at the TV. Dare put Venom in the Figure-Four, and that was it.

"They rerun tapes all the time," she said. "This looks like last month's Bone-Breaker Blast." Then she sputtered. "Goddamn Dare. He's such a pompous ass. You should've seen the guy tonight back at the room."

"I'm glad that I didn't."

"The motherfucker didn't even come. Fucked me steady for a solid hour and couldn't shoot his load. What a waste of hard dick."

Straker gulped. Her slow-but-sure reversion to profanity shocked him, but what shocked him even more was the information. What normal man wouldn't be able to achieve orgasm with such a woman? The idea seemed preposterous.

"But at least I found out that the rumor is true."

"What rumor?" he asked, unable to take his eyes off her terry-covered rump as she stood aside from the set.

"He's hung like a horse. Nine and a half inches."

Straker gulped again. *That's a third more than I got, the son of a bitch!*

"But don't feel insecure," she went on. "What good is a gun that doesn't shoot?"

"I don't have anything to feel insecure about," he insisted, now hating Dare even more for his endowment.

"I wasn't implying that you do. It's just real funny how men get all uptight about guys with bigger penises."

"Hey, I may not have the Loch Ness Monster in my pants, but at least mine works."

"Oh, I'm quite convinced of that. The toilet and wastebasket back at my other motel are convinced too."

Straker reddened like a beet. *She'll never let me forget that one.* She giggled again, then traipsed back and forth, sipping her drink, then coming back to watch the TV. Now Dare was doing one of his rants to the microphone. Woo this and woo that. Stylin' and profilin' *Jesus,* Straker thought, totally enshrouded in despair.

"Do me a favor, will you? And don't take this the wrong way." Quite suddenly, she sat on the floor before the couch. Right between Straker's knees. "Would you rub my shoulders?"

Straker nearly spat out his beer. "Uh, yeah. Sure."

He had to catch his breath; suddenly here she was, so calmly sitting between his legs, sipping her spiked Coke and watching the tv. Almost like... *Like boyfriend and girlfriend. Like husband and wife,* he thought. But that was nonsense, another errant fantasy, a 13-year-old musing about the girl next door who dated jocks. His fingers trembled like delirium tremens when he reached forward and touched her shoulders. He was oblivious now, he was elsewhere. He gently squeezed her shoulder muscles and nearly ejaculated when she moaned.

"God, that feels good," she breathed.

Touching her warm skin sent Straker to another plane of existence. He wanted to cry, she was so beautiful. Her skin like damp silk, the soap-scent lifting off her, the devastating cleavage he could see as the towel stretched across her bosom.

*I would do anything for you,* he mused.

He knew that if he even so much as brushed his crotch, he'd come. No doubt about it. He was so hard now it hurt. So hard he thought his dick might bust out of his jeans and start to dance. His mind struggled for discourse...

"So what was the big revelation? What principle evidence did the Wonder Boy give you?"

"We know they go to a You-Store-It in Big Stone gap," she said.

He didn't argue this time—he was too pent up rubbing her shoulders. Her dry hair shined over his hands.

"I—" She propped her arms up on his thighs, laxed back till her head nearly lay in his crotch. "That feels sooooo good." Was it his imagination or could he actually see her nipples distending beneath the bath towel? *Don't be an asshole,* he told himself. *She no more attracted to me than than to a pile of bricks. I ain't got the muscles. I ain't got the bleach-blond hair and the nine and a half inch dick. I don't style and I don't profile.* Here was the closest he'd ever get to his dream: rubbing her shoulders. Straker doubted that he'd ever been more depressed in his life. Yet he considered it a privilege just to be able to touch her, just to knead her shoulders and have contact.

*Beggars can't be choosers,* he reasoned.

She took another sip of her drink. "All this shit I've said about wrestlers being hot? Sure, they're good looking guys but when you get right down to it, they're all a bunch of assholes."

Straker tensed. It was almost as if she'd read his mood like a psychic.

"They're all the biggest losers you could ever meet. Selfish, pretentious, arrogant. They think they're hot shit because they can dive off the ropes and pile-drive and suplex and bodyslam. They think that their big pecs and big dicks make them men. They're not *real* men. They're carnival freaks of the new age. Most of them can barely sign their names on their paychecks. There's more to a man than a big cock."

Straker kneaded on. Yeah, that Everclear was loosening her up, all right. "But you're attracted to them. Admit it."

"Sure. And are you gonna tell me that you're not attracted to the average silicone-filled porn star or Playboy bunny? It's the same thing only in reverse. All body, no brains. Most of these grapplers'd be cleaning the grease pit at McDonald's if it weren't for wrestling. It gets to the point where you...despise them, for wasting their lives on this charade. True, in a real fight, most of them could kick ass. Most of them could take on a pro boxer on the street and win—but what does that mean?"

# GOON

Straker didn't care. His balls felt big as cueballs; his cock was about to spurt, bust, and die.

"So you're telling me that..." He paused, reflecting. "You've never had an orgasm with any of these guys?"

"Nope." Her eyes closed against the attentions of his fingers. "But I'll tell you one thing," she went on. "If we weren't both professionals...I'd want to—"

Straker froze. He knew what she was about to say, and in spite of his disbelief he even supposed he knew what was coming. "Oh, fuck it," she dismissed. She stood up, dropped her towel, and straddled him on the couch. "What the hell, right?"

"Uh. Right."

Straker came in his pants. He shivered beneath her as she pressed her breasts to his face. Her mouth opened over his, her tongue plunging. This was too much, too soon, but Straker wasn't going to complain. She was an angel of flesh come to absolve him. Her arms girded him, squeezing, and she torqued him out flat on the couch, then indecorously grabbed his hand and planted it on her sex. *Yep,* he thought. *She uses that hair remover for more than her legs.* Her pubis was bald as a baby's proverbial backside, flawlessly so. Not even a nub. It was fascinatingly erotic.

"You're really turning me on," her hot breath gusted into his mouth. "Put your finger right...right—"

Straker's beeper went off in his back pocket. *Oh for shit sake! What is this—Hill Street Fuckin' Blues?* She giggled in his mouth. "Aren't you going to answer it?"

"Hell no!" he replied, roaming his hands over her. Then the beeping stopped. "See. Wrong number."

"Do like you were—" She squeezed tighter against him, opened her legs. Just as his finger touched her clitoris—

"God damn!"

—the beeper went off again.

"I swear to God my clitoris isn't connected to your beeper," she laughed. She lounged back. "Go answer it. It's probably someone from your office."

Straker ground his teeth together and got up from the couch.

"Collier, I should've known," he said when he saw the number on the Motorola pager. He had to walk funny to the phone, and the recent deposit of semen only intensified the discomfort. He nearly punched holes in the phone when he dialed.

"What do you want?" he sniped when Deputy Chief Sidney Collier answered. "Do you have any idea what you—"

Collier didn't lolligag on the other end. "Shut up and listen. Luntville police—rube department, backwoods town clowns, just wired the VCU with a doozy—those crackers found about two dozen dead bodies near the county line. Like a mass grave, they said it was; somebody's been throwing these bodies in it for months. It took the Hazmat Team two hours just to get a body count."

"Luntville?" Straker blinked. "A mass grave." *What the fuck's he talking about?*

"Jan Beck inspected the scene," Collier went on with no explanation. "The 64s on the bottom had congealed into a mass of, and I quote, 'putrefactive effluvium.' We're talking a trench full of dead bodies, maggots, and slime."

Straker could not dissimulate. Thirty seconds ago he'd been about to make love to the woman of his dreams, and now his boss was telling him about…putrefactive effluvium? This did not relate.

"You blow your brain out your nose the last time you sneezed?" Collier inquired. "I just told you we found a mass grave in Luntville, and you're not saying anything."

Straker shook his head. To hell with protect and serve—he wanted to get laid. "All right, boss, that's a terrible human tragedy, but what in the living *fuck* has it got to do with me? I'm on a totally different case."

"Think again, nitz. All the victims were male, late 20s, early 30s, and according to Beck and the TSD team, they'd all been, and I qoute, 'divorced of their reproductive organs via a mode of expeditious dentation.' To put it more bluntly, all these guys they found in the hole had their cocks bitten off."

Straker's eyes opened at the grotesqurie, yet his sentience remained fully disassociated, musing of Melinda: drunk and horny, and eager for him. "DC, I still don't see what this has to do with my case—"

"It has plenty to do with it, nibblenuts, because after we ran down

IDs on the victims we discovered they all had one thing in common. They were all wrestling groupies—*male* wrestling groupies. Sound familiar?"

Straker's mouth opened, closed, then opened again. "So you're saying that our primary suspect—"

"Yeah, this Goon motherfucker—looks like he's swinging both ways, doing the job on the chicks *and* these guys."

*Yes, yes, but*— A stalling thought, then Straker proposed, "It doesn't make much sense, does it, I mean from an evidence perspective? The m.o.s are totally different, not to mention that he's disposing of the women in a totally different manner from the way he's disposing of the men."

"You think I give a shit?" Collier spat back. "This case just doubled in the headache department, and there's something else."

"Yeah?"

"Are you with Melinda Pierce?"

"Uh, yeah, DC. We were just going over, uh, critical points regarding the Bilks murder."

"Right. At four in the morning."

"We're dedicated."

"Well put your pants back on and get ready for another bombshell."

*I didn't have time to get them off, thanks to you, you weasel, you schmuck, you—*

"Melinda Pierce ain't no reporter," Collier returned. "I just got a call from my buddy at the paper and he said he's never heard of her. She's faking her credentials, must be some kind of wacko police buff or something, but get her the hell out of there. We don't need some civilian nutcase screwing up the investigation."

Straker's jaw fell open. "There's—" He glanced at her. She lay back oblivious on the couch, casually naked, her ankles crossed and her hair spilling over her shoulders. She was waiting for him, waiting for him to come back to her.

"It's no joke, lover boy," Collier went on. "I don't know what the hell's going on. Just kick her ass out of there. We don't even have time to fool around with an obstruction charge."

"But-but-but—"

"Do it. That's an order. Then get your swinging dick back to HQ for the new prelims and division of record files."

Straker turned again to glance at her but she wasn't there.

All he heard after that was a loud *clunk!* He saw a lamp fall to the floor, and then realized what the clunk had been: the lamp impacting his head. Then his mind winked out.

# PART FOUR

He awoke to the sound of hammering. After a moment he realized it was a combination of a fist repeatedly hitting the door and a much duller but more insistent pounding between his ears. Struggling to his feet he got to the door and threw it open to see two uniformed cops.

"Captain Straker, I'm Officer Mason and this is Officer Adams. We've been sent to assist with the bust or to relieve you if you're not up to continuing."

"I'll be fine," Straker lied. "We have a general idea where they're at, we just need to check the You-Store-It in Big Stone Gap. We'll take my car, it'll attract less attention. It's about a three and half hour drive. So some on."

✪ — ✪ — ✪

When they arrived in Big Stone Gap, it was nearing 3:00 in the afternoon. Straker was almost beside himself after a gruellingly long drive where Mason and Adams had, ironicaly, talked of nothing but pro-wrestling. It was no small wonder that Adams was still in a uniform after seventeen years in law enforcement. The idiot actually thought it was for real. Mason was even worse: he had a memory for matches and past angles that bordered on idiot-savant. Straker had heard more about the history of the Deep South Wrestling TV Title Belt than any sane person would ever want to know.

Straker then met for an hour with the locals. A brusk Sheriff Tanner had a force of two deputies, giving them a total of six men to arrest what might prove to be the most dangerous serial-killer in the South. He wondered where Melinda was...and what was her angle in this; with her passion for sex, could it be that's why she wanted to get to Goon before they did?

"The warehouses are out here on the edge of town," said Tanner, jarring Straker out of his thoughts of Melinda's perfect body. "We go in after it gets dark, see if we can catch these sick fucks with anything that will incriminate them. What with all the missing body parts, it's a safe bet they've got trophies stashed in the warehouse."

"We'll split into three teams, so we're each paired up with one of the local guys who knows the town. All the storage places are on a four block stretch here." Tanner pointed to the map. "Straker, you go solo, but get these guys in there as soon as you see anything; and you guys pair up, and we'll just work our way to center. As soon as you spot either one of these guys or even think you do, call for backup. We don't want to fuck this up and have anyone get hurt. Do I hafta remind any-one about all those guys found with their dicks bitten off?"

Straker had a sick feeling that five well-armed men were terribly outnumbered by what they were going after...

*A You-Store-It?* That's what Melinda had said at the motel; Straker had gotten the address she'd circled in the phone book.

And that was the sign he saw from the end of the road. These joints were all over the place. Twenty bucks a month to rent a storage garage. First thing he saw in the main lot was a long row of garages. And the second thing...

A black Winnabego sat parked in the otherwise empty lot.

None of this made sense but he didn't care. He soft-stepped past the sign, wisked around the back of the mobile home, and paused. *No gun,* he realized, patting his pants. He winced at the tacky sensation of semen in his shorts. *Christ, if I get killed, Jan Beck'll have a good old laugh once she gets me into the morgue.* But he had to think. What was going on?

A light shone through the Winnabego's window. He listened at the door for a full minute, heard nothing, then entered. A small rear room showed him nothing out of the ordinary, just—

*Wait a minute...*

On a supply shelf he found a box of SKIN SMOOTH hair remover, the same brand he'd seen in Melinda's travel case. Weird. What would a wrestler be doing with something like that? But a more grim discovery came next: a cardboard box on the floor full of beige plastic shower curtains, the same kind all of the bodies had been found wrapped up in. Then he heard a groan.

Straker grabbed a metal flashlight from a rack, the only weapon available, then approached the curtain before him. He quickly whipped it back and saw—

"Felander," he said.

On the floor a husky guy with a black goatee groaned again, holding his head. "Oh, man. Who are you?"

"State police. Where's Melinda?"

Felander winced to lean up. "Christ, that bitch hits hard."

"You don't have to tell me. What's going on?"

"Look, I had no choice. It was Kevin's fault, he's the one that had the book."

"Book? What are you talking about?"

"The grimoire, one of those devil-worship things Kevin collected—Kevin the Druid.

*Kevin the Druid,* Straker recalled. Melinda had mentioned him, and so had Traci Wilcox. *A wrestler who'd disappeared without a trace.*

"He was really into all that occult shit—it wasn't just a work. Him and me and three ringrats, we were all fucked up one night and just fooling around and somebody suggested we try one of the spells, and Goon is what we got."

"Are you trying to tell Goon is some kind of demon?"

"I don't know what you call him, all I know is that after we did what the book said, Kevin and the girls were ripped to pieces and this thing is telling me I have to help him out or get torn up like the others. What the fuck would you do? So we made a deal. I keep him isolated in the truck, drive him to the cards and set up the promotion, and he let's me keep the cash. And in between…he does the girls."

Straker paled, thinking of Melinda; he had to find Goon first before anything happened to her. "*Does* as in *murders*. You've been harboring a criminal. You're guilty of accessory murder. Where's Melinda Pierce?

She came here a little while ago looking for Goon? If we can get to him, there might not be any more innocent victims!"

"Innocent victims? Melinda? You don't get it do you? When we cast that spell, there were two of those things…" Felander offered a forlorn glance. "Melinda's the other one."

Straker looked around and shivered. Melinda, the most beautiful woman he'd ever seen. The same as this monster…

"They get off on it," Felander said, "sex, killing, drugs, just like the ones here. The only difference is that it's been six months, and Goon told me that for some reason only one of them could exist here longer than that. They're having a fucking contest! Goon didn't do all those guys they found in that pit. It was Melinda…"

Straker felt his balls shrivel to the size of chickpeas. He thought of the corpses with their penises missing. Bitten off.

"One of them has to go back tonight. They're from someplace else, Hell or whatever you want to call it. Melinda came here looking for Goon so they can have it out. The stronger one is going to get to stay here and keep killing, the other one has to go back. Where they come from, they're bored. That's why all the sex, drugs, booze and everything, they're like the worst of our own scumbags and thrill-killers. Goon was their equivalent to a pathological serial-killer and Melinda is just as dangerous."

Straker sat wearied on the edge of the bed, listening to this guy. He thought he'd heard everything. But with no gun and no cuffs, what was he going to do with him?

Felander went on with his pitch. "They're probably inside the garage, but I wouldn't go in there for anything, not with both of them there."

"Supernatural serial-killers, huh?" Straker just shook his head. "Demons having a duel to see who gets to stay here and slaughter more people? That's just great."

"Don't believe me, go look."

"Oh, you're sure they're here?"

Felander jerked his thumb. "In the garage. Because of the spell we couldn't get too far from here—the incarnation point. That's why we've stayed in this territory instead of going to one of the big federations. Goon likes to come back here every few days. I don't know why Melinda never did, but I think she might be the stronger of the two."

Straker sighed. "All right, let me get this straight for the record. You conjured up a pair of demons in a You-Store-It, and you put one of them in professional wrestling and the other disappears and resurfaces masquerading as a reporter? That makes sense to me."

"It does if you think about it. Regional wrestling? It's perfect. He's the ultimate heel. He can't be hurt, so the gimmick is a real grabber. DDT the guy, run his face into a steel ringpost, break a bat over his head. The fans love it. He looks so good in the ring I could get him a million a year with WCW."

"Then why didn't you?"

"Too much exposure, man. In a big fed he'd have to travel all over the country. He'd be all over television. And the more exposure, the riskier it is with the ringrats. DSWC? It's just a bunch of redneck towns and little arenas. A ringrat disappears every week or so, nobody gives a shit. Some drunken cracker vanishes after a match, no one even looks. It's too obscure. But you start leaving mutilated bodies around the big card cities, then that's another story. It'd be too difficult to manage. But down here everything's cool, and the money's not bad."

"So why does he rape and kill these girls?"

"'Cos he's a thrill-junkie. What more reason do you need? He's Jack the Ripper from another dimension. He does a girl a week, I get rid of the bodies, and that's that." Felander smirked, then sputtered. "But he always told me Melinda might come after him."

"To fight it out to see who stays and who goes back to Hell?"

"Right."

"She's a demon, and so is Goon?"

"You got it."

*This guy actually believes this bullshit,* Straker could tell. He sighed again. "In Melinda's travel bag I saw a box of hair-remover, then I come in here an see the same thing."

"Their bodies look just like ours," Felander explained. "I mean, you saw the chick—she's a knockout."

"Tell me about it," Straker said.

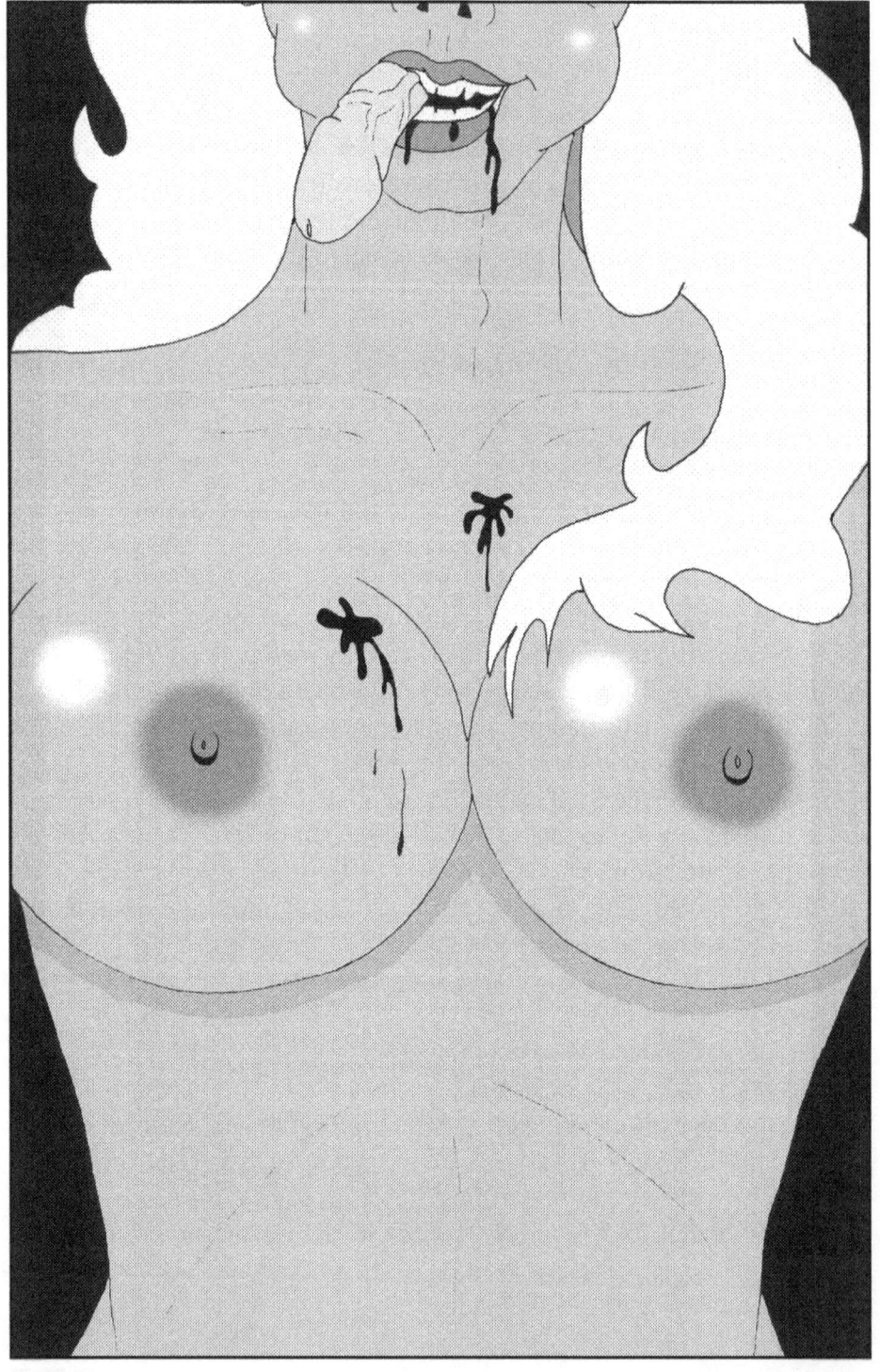

"But their eyes are different—they're yellow. So they have to wear designer contacts."

Straker paused. Hadn't he also seen a contact lens case in her travel bag?

"And they're hair is, like, this really weird brownish-green color, the color of creek water sort of, and it won't take to the hair dyes we got here. So every couple of days Goon spreads this hair-remover all over himself, burns it off."

"But Melinda's hair is blond."

Felander shrugged again. "It's a wig, man."

Delusional people often believed their own delusions, Straker knew. Felander had an answer for everything, mad as it all was. *He acts and sounds like he's telling the truth because he actually believes that he is.*

"You got a mobile phone in this house on wheels?"

"The chick busted it when she came in here." Felander pointed to the pieces. "She also took the keys. Then she put the screws on me to verify that Goon was in the garage. I gave her the unit number, then she punched my lights out."

"Well, look, I've got to take you in," Straker said.

Felander stood up. He was big. "With what? That flashlight?"

"You can go hard or easy."

"Look, man. I don't want trouble. My gig is washed up now. There's never going to be any evidence left of Goon, so what do you care? I'm booking."

"Don't test me, Felander," Straker tried to sound tough. No cuffs. No radio for backup. *I'll have to tie the guy up,* Straker deduced.

Felander must've seen it coming. "I'm a pacifist by nature, but...I used to wrestle too."

Straker swung the flashlight toward his unwitting foe's head. Next thing he knew, Felander had him in a chicken wing. Straker howled. Then the belly-to-back suplex lifted Straker up, feet kicking, then dropped the back of his head on the Winnebago's floor—BAM!

Groaning, he looked up through a half-conscious veil and saw Felander run off into the twilight-tinged woods.

❋ — ❋ — ❋

Goon was close by.

Melinda could sense his aura in the air.

She stalked in silence through the barely lit warehouse interior. Anticipating the confrontation enflamed her—her breasts tingled, her nipples felt hard as small stones and stuck out as much. Primal excitement hummed in the already drenched cleft between her legs.

"Bitch," came the sibilant whisper.

Then the enormous figure stepped out from behind a stack of crates.

Goon was still wearing his ring attire. Flat, dead eyes regarded her impassively from the tight mask.

Melinda's sexual juices began to run like an open tap just looking at him, and Goon was obviously just as excited by the sight of Melinda. His massive erection looked like a stiff serpent in his trunks.

Even though there could only be room for one of them on this plane of existence, Melinda would miss Goon terribly. Their previous sexual encounters had been explosive fuckfests that had lasted for days. The only thing that seemed to come close to being as satisfying was the tremendous rush she'd gotten from some of the redneck male ringrats she'd snagged after the matches.

Not having sex with them.

Killing them.

Gnawing their cocks off just as they'd ejaculate down her throat. Like biting into an eclair still warm from the oven, savoring all that hot filling. The sensation was electric in its intensity: the sudden gust of blood splashing into her mouth never failed to produce the wildest orgasm.

She ate them up like appetizers.

Sex with Goon, on the other hand, was something that could never happen again. It was time for one of them to go back, and Melinda had come too far to fail now.

"I'm going to beat you senseless and send you back," hissed the masked monster, and without further warning he launched a drop-kick at her head. The panther-like agility was terrifying in a man of this size, but Melinda nimbly ducked under the kick and caught Goon in a vicious armbar.

Dropping quickly to his knees, Goon pulled Melinda off balance, dislodging her grip. He caught her around the waist and hoisted her into the air in prelude to an Atomic Drop. With 350 pounds of weight focused, he slammed her down feet-first, jolting her crotch against his knee. The pain was nearly paralyzing. Melinda felt as though her spine had compressed into a solid mass; she was helpless as the behemoth seized her wrist and Irish-Whipped her into a stack of crates.

She hit shoulder-first, the crates blowing apart in a shower of slats and splintered wood.

Goon chuckled.

Melinda struggled to her feet, grabbing a two-and-a-half-foot slat in the process.

She feined exhaustion but as he reached to grab her, she whacked the piece of wood in a swift arc across his face. Blood spurted from the suddenly crushed nose; he reeled backwards. Now Melinda pivoted and launched herself toward him in a hand-spring elbow. Goon caught the blow full in the sternum and crashed back into more crates.

Pursuing the advantage, Melinda swept Goon's pillar-like legs out from under him, and leaped to finish him off.

Skyrockets exploded behind her eyes as the size 15 foot came up and caught her square in the jaw. Melinda nearly blacked out from the impact. Two massive arms encircled her as she felt herself being lifted and spun into a belly to belly suplex; she could feel the gorged cock pressed against her leg.

Goon was getting off on this. She knew that if he succeeded in beating her, not only would she be returned to Hell, every orifice of her unconscious body would first be plundered.

Shaking off vertigo, she saw through glazing eyes the huge man preparing to spring on her with a crushing knee-drop. At the last possible instant, she rolled out of the way, letting the monster drive his knee into the concrete flooring. As he howled, Melinda used the precious moments to regain her breath. But Goon was back up fast, charging at her with his head lowered like a battering ram, intent on driving her into the wall.

She knew she couldn't take a blow of such force.

*This is it,* she thought.

She sidestepped, caught Goon around the neck while kicking her heels high into the air. The move allowed her drive the top of his head into the concrete—a perfectly executed DDT. She sprang up, primed herself for another attack.

But none came.

Goon lay unconscious, a defeated hulk.

❊ — ❊ — ❊

The You-Store-It existed as a complex of long brick buildings sectioned off into separate storage garages. Straker, headache thudding, walked the entire complex and saw no evidence of Melinda nor Goon. But towards the end of the last building, one of the garage doors stood open.

Straker walked in, splaying his flashlight.

The unit was quiet as the proverbial tomb. A massive figure lay prone on the floor.

Then someone stepped out from the shadows: Melinda looking strangely taller and more powerfully built, just larger somehow, but still the most beautiful woman Straker had ever seen.

"Felander said you were…"

"Demons, for lack of a better term," she acknowledged. "I'm just the same as you, I do what makes me feel good."

Straker's flashlight beam strayed past her to the pentagram on the floor. "And that…is what you're going to send Goon back with?"

"Yep. It's what we came here through."

Maybe twenty feet from point to point the pentagram was painted on the garage floor with what appeared to be red paint, but Straker suspected was something far more sinister.

"Your investigation is over Captain, Goon'll be gone. You'll never say anything to anyone about this because no one would believe it. I'm going to walk out of here without killing you because I sort of like you. You're kind of amusing, what with your jacking off every time you see me."

"This is unbelievable," Straker murmured. "I must be on drugs."

"Look." She pinched the contact lenses out of her eyes. The irsises glittered like yellow sparkle. "Still don't believe me?" She dragged off the blond wig. Even bald she was beautiful, even with the horrible yellow eyes. Her rump stretched the back of her denim skirt when she leaned over. "Remember when we were at the arena? Here's the real reason I couldn't let Goon see me then. Let's just say it would've been instant recognition."

She tugged on Goon's mask till it peeled off. Straker expected something more clichéd—something hideous, a monster's face. Anything but this.

Goon's face was identical to Melinda's.

"We all have identical facial features," she told him, flinging the mask aside. "We distinguish each other's individuality via ocular emmissions. Where I come from, every female looks just like me, and every male looks just like him."

She smiled at Straker. "Help me get him inside the pentagram, will you?"

Straker dumbly obeyed. *I'm helping a demon sex-killer send another demon back to Hell. It doesn't get any crazier than this,* he thought. They each grabbed a foot and dragged. "Christ, this big son of a bitch weighs more than a fucking piano," she commented.

*And I love the way she talks!*

"It's been real, Captain," she said a moment later. "Get out of here now, all right? I gotta go."

Straker felt appalled. "So that's it? You just send him back and you disappear? What makes you think I can let you do that?"

Melinda shuddered and seemed to grow somehow, the yellow eyes practically glowing. "Captain, what makes you think you could stop me? Remember those guys in the pit? I'm going to leave this area completely, and you don't know where I'm going. Be smart and just forget everything you saw."

"But what the hell do I tell my boss?"

"I wouldn't tell him anything unless you want to wind up in the Rubber Ramada. Just forget about it. I'm sending Goon where he belongs. And I'm sorry if this screws up your job, but at least you're not going to be finding any more bodies here. I apologize for dumping them all in your jurisdiction. You know. Shit happens."

*You ain't kidding.*

She smiled at him, her yellow eyes sparkling. "It was fun doing this gig with you." She hitched up her halter. "Too bad your beeper went off when it did. We would've had some mondo sex."

Straker continued to stare. *I've got the hots for a demon,* he thought absurdly.

"Well," he said just as absurdly. "We still can."

"Nope. Like I said, I gotta get this big lug home."

"But…Melinda." Straker's eyes grew wide as coins when he realized what he was about to say. "I-I-I…"

"Give me a break!" she complained. "Don't say something you'll regret."

"I've got an idea!" he enthused. "A way that we can be together!"

That's what he said, but this is what he was thinking: *I love her… I'm in love with a demon…*

"Jesus," she chuckled. "You mortals really are something. So give me a good laugh—what's this big idea of yours?"

# EPILOGUE

Alan McLaughlin took another hit from his pint of Bacardi, glancing around to see if he'd been observed by either of the two security guards. They were both busy trying to eject some crazy who had tried to vault into the ring. Yeah the Island County Coliseum was jumping tonight, that was for sure. The Pacific Northwest Wrestling Alliance always brought out the rowdies.

As Alan took another hit from the pint, the announcer called out the third match of the evening, this was what he'd been waiting for, the reason he'd paid a guy ten bucks to swap seats so he could be right on the aisle near ringside where the wrestlers entered.

"Hailing from the slopes of Mount Kilamanjaro, she is the current Pacific Northwest Women's Wrestling Champion, Kimali!" intoned the announcer as a very large black woman approached the ring snarling and spitting at fans. "And her opponent this evening, the number-one ranked contender for the Pacific Northwest Women's Wrestling Championship, hailing from parts unknown… The Magnificent Melinda!"

Now this was one hot babe! Tall, blonde, and rumor had it very available. Alan thought he caught her eye and a hint of a smile as Melinda got into the ring.

The action started immediately with Melinda launching a drop kick toward the larger woman's head. Kimali sidestepped with a display of speed that was remarkable in a woman of her size and caught the challenger in a belly-to-back suplex that shook the ring. Kimali then climbed to the second rope launching herself onto the prone wrestler with a vicious splash. The ref got as far as a two-count before

Magnificent Melinda got a shoulder off the mat. Alan felt himself getting hard just looking at Melinda's perfect body. Both women were now out of the ring trading open handed slaps as the referee began his interminably slow ten-count; Melinda had just grabbed a chair from a fan and lifted it high to deliver the coup de grace to the champion... Alan had seen them do this finish before in the match at Western Washington Sports Complex last week, and sure enough with perfect timing, Kimali punched Melinda in the stomach and with one smooth motion snatched the chair away from her and—WHAAACK!— brought it down with full force across Melinda's head, dropping to her to the floor.

That was that.

After an explosion of applause, two pencil-neck geeks carried Melinda off on a stretcher.

*Jesus,* Alan thought. *What I wouldn't do for a night with her...*

"Like the action?" a voice inquired.

Alan turned to face some guy in a hokey glitter-jacket, like that shit Freddie Blassie used to where back before he turned a hundred. Alan had seen this dude at some other matches too, now that he thought of it.

"I got a funny feeling that Melinda's hot for you."

"Oh, yeah?" Alan replied. "Any woman in her right mind's got the hots for me, pal. Who are you?"

"I'm Straker the Sinister," the guy said. "Melinda's manager. "Trust me." Then he winked and put something into Alan's hand.

A motel-room key.

*Looks like this is going to be my lucky night,* Alan thought.

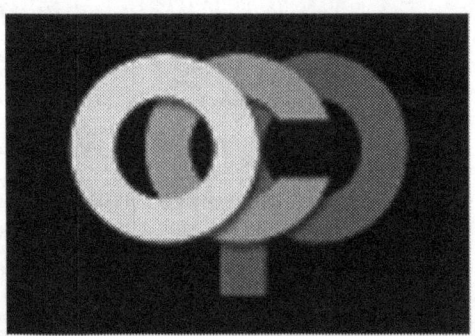

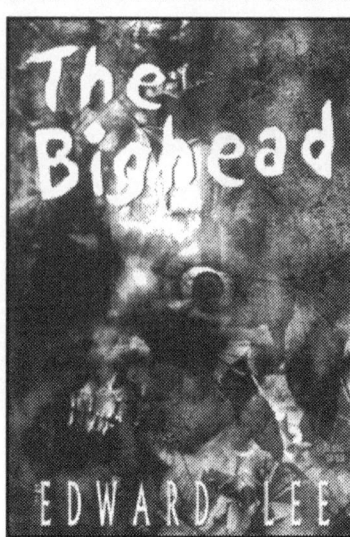

www.ingramcontent.com/pod-product-compliance
Lightning Source LLC
Chambersburg PA
CBHW051841170626
46807CB00003B/1281